BEFORE YOU READ

What you are about to read is an erotic fantasy romance intended exclusively for an 18+ audience.

It contains explicit language and adult situations, as well as graphic depictions of consensual sex with three adults, six arms, eight tentacles, four legs, three anal cavities, and...

No partridge in a pear tree. That would have made things *awkward*.

Please read responsibly, and always practice safe hex.

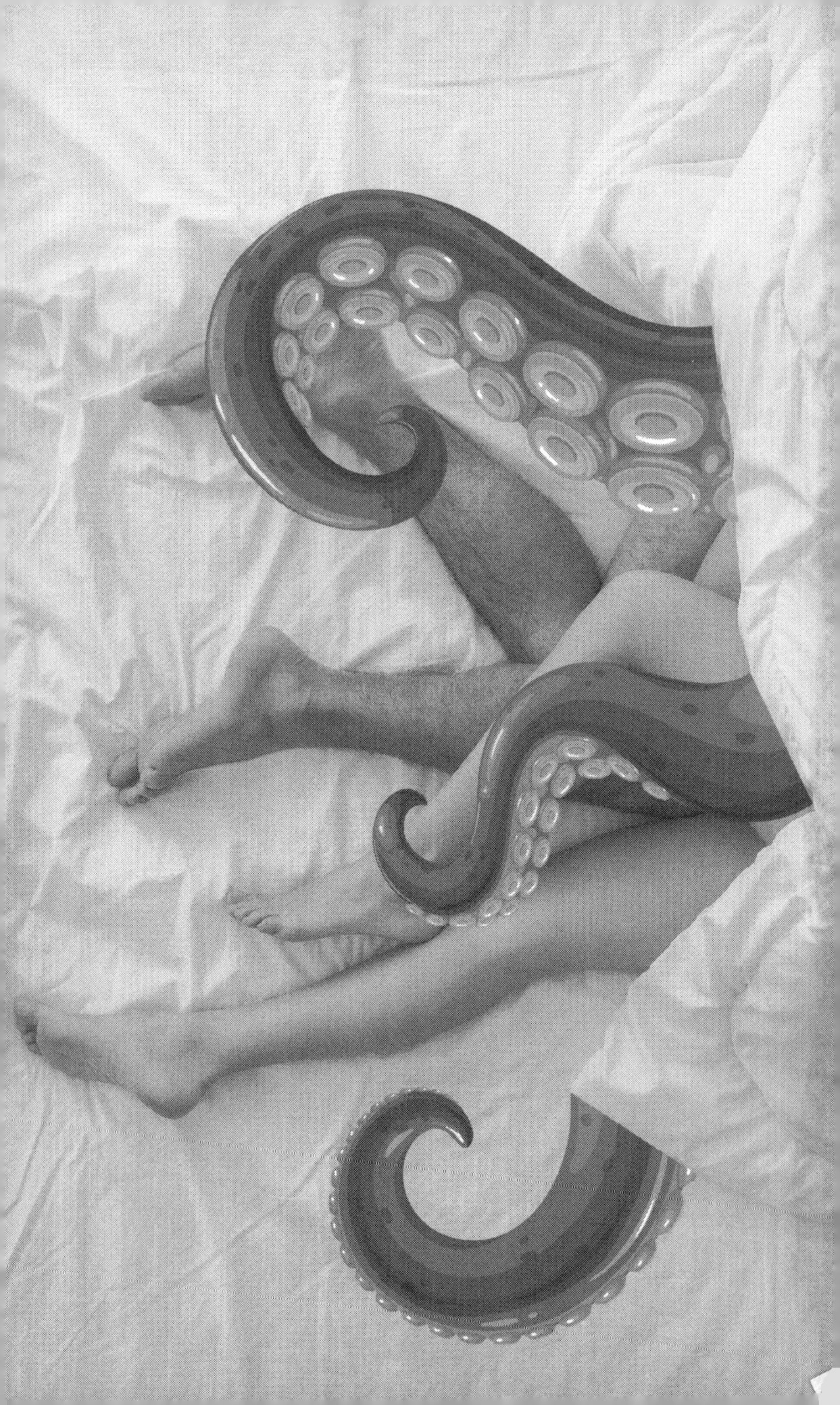

TINSEL & Tentacles

MONSTER MASH HOLIDAY STORY

KATE McDARRIS

Copyright © 2022 by Kate McDarris

All rights reserved.

This book or any portion thereof may not be reproduced or used in any manner whatsoever without the express written permission of the publisher, except for the use of brief quotations in a book review.

This book is a work of fiction. References to real people, events, establishments, organizations, or locations are intended only to provide a sense of authenticity, and are used fictitiously. All other characters, and all incidents and dialogue, are drawn from the author's imagination and are not to be construed as real.

This book is for Mikayla, who predicted tentacles would be all the rage this holiday season.

CHAPTER ONE

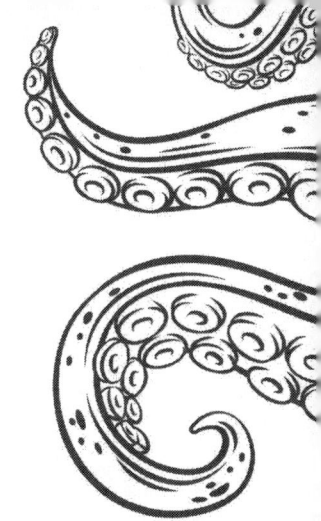

THE MANAGER

"I KNOW, mom. It's a busy time is all." I stand at the door with the phone crammed up between my ear and my shoulder, juggling the hotel key and a tray with three coffees.

"But you're already in New York. Can't you just come up for the day? A few hours." My mother's pitch turns higher and her voice gets watery. "It could be Gran's last Christmas."

"You've been saying that every year for the past decade." I readjust the coffees and knock on the door with my boot.

"Yes, and at some point it really will be." My mother sighs and her voice clears in an instant when she realizes I won't be convinced. "And then you'll feel terrible."

"Granny understands. She'd be grumpy if I showed up there instead of, you know, doing my actual job that I get paid for." I manage to get the keycard in the door but don't slide it out quickly enough and it blinks red. "Fuck."

"Fucking language, darling." My mother sips her

morning coffee loudly and I clench my shoulder to keep the phone from sliding out and dropping to the floor. The last thing I need to deal with is trying to get a shattered screen replaced on the last big shopping day before Christmas. I pound the door again with my foot. "What's that noise?"

"Mom, this really isn't a good time. We're on a tight schedule." I finally grow a brain and put the coffee tray down on the floor. Then I try the keycard again and it still doesn't work.

"Yes, yes, I know. Busy and important things." She sounds annoyed but I can hear the smile on her face through the line. "Can't be easy managing the way you do, Marci. You take very good care of him."

"It isn't and I do. I'm paid very well for it." I wince quickly. "Not that the money is why I do it. I love taking care of him, seriously. I only mean—"

"It's your job." Mom softens. "Why don't you bring him with you? You know he likes my cookies."

"Aside from the fact I wouldn't dare impose the absolute madness of a Collins Family Christmas on him, it would be a security nightmare. Everyone would have to sign an NDA. Ryder would have an aneurism." I check the room number on the keycard and roll my eyes. I dig in my pocket and find the correct one. The light blinks green and the lock clicks. "Bingo!"

"I've got to go, Mom." I grab the handle and brace my foot against the door to keep it from swinging shut. Then I call out into the massive suite. "Barney, you up?"

"I know, but I miss you. What's on the schedule for today?" She has no intention of dropping off that easily.

I'm going to have to pry her off the call with a crowbar, as usual.

"Ah, rehearsals for tonight. An interview, then the concert." I bend over to grab the coffees while I balance against the heavy door. Ryder, our head of security, appears down the hall and jogs the last few steps toward me.

"Morning." He dips his chiseled chin and his strong fingers brush over the back of my hand when he relieves me of the coffee tray.

My stomach fizzes with that light ticklish feeling I've been getting around him lately.

"Thanks. Morning." I point to the phone and silently mouth the word, *mom*. His rich brown eyes sparkle with understanding. That little dimple appears right in the corner of his mouth. *Mmph.*

He leans in and—fuck, he smells good. Like some kind of spicy pine forest, and *muscles*.

"Hi, Mrs. Collins."

"Oh, is that Ryder? Tell him I've almost got his sweater finished. I wasn't expecting it to take this long, but he's so broad through the chest. You're sure those measurements you sent were correct?" My mother emphasizes those last few words and my cheeks warm as I follow him into the luxurious hotel suite. "It's like I'm knitting a quilt."

"Oh. I'm sure." I stare at those enormous shoulders live and up close in glorious detail. My gaze travels down his body, to his dark jeans and the perfectly sculpted ass and muscular thighs he's managed to pour into them.

Damn.

The door bangs shut behind me and I startle. Ryder places the coffees on the table, jumping to attention at the loud noise. Always on alert. So protective.

I fight back a moan.

"Marci?" I realize mom's still speaking. "Are you going to ask about Christmas?"

I frown. "No, Mom. It's not possible. We're off to London for New Year's right after the show."

"Up and at 'em, Barns!" Ryder uses his security voice. The one that makes people jump to attention and obey him immediately. The one that makes my heart stutter.

"Ooh, are you doing the Morning Show with Gayle and Gregg? Will you meet them?" She perks up. "Tell them I said hi. Do you think they're *involved*? I've always felt like there was some chemistry there."

I can't hold back my smile. My mother acts as if everyone appearing on a screen is her own personal best friend. "I don't know, mom. I've really got to go now. We have to get Barney up and go over logistics for the day."

It wouldn't be the first time we've had to drag the sleepy rockstar out of bed.

Ryder slips into the bedroom and comes straight back out. His usual deep golden complexion drains to a washed out gray.

My throat clenches with sudden anxiety.

I rush into the bedroom. The bed is rumpled and empty. "Where—?"

A thousand terrible headlines bolt through my mind. Barney Myles has never been one to abuse any substances or have any trouble with drinking or anything else along those lines. As far as world-famous, chart-topping musicians go, he's actually pretty boring and extremely private.

Perhaps a bit anxious at times, but who wouldn't be in that position? The crowds and photographers can get out of control extremely quickly. Not to mention there's always a spectacle wherever he goes. His fans are dedicated and rabid, but mostly in a positive way.

I spin around and discover a window between the bedroom and bathroom overlooking the massive marble tub. The narrow panels are half open revealing the view straight inside.

My chin unhinges.

Suddenly, I can't even get enough air in my lungs to make a sound. All I can do is stand there and stare, for how long I have no idea.

I'm mesmerized. Hypnotized. Captivated. Whatever.

On the other side of the window, Barney Myles, voted sexiest man alive multiple times, is in the giant soaking tub.

A set of long, glossy pink and purple marbled tentacles rise up from the mountain of bubbles.

His eyes are shut and there's a little grin curving his full mouth upward. The tentacles sway and bop jauntily to whatever music he's got playing in his ear-pods. It's the lightest and happiest I've seen him in... years.

That warm tickle in my lower belly that Ryder ignited grows and spreads, melting further down in a liquid heat that pools right between my legs.

One of the tentacles slaps up against the window in a heavy thud. Little suckers press into the glass, wet and slick, wiggling to a beat only Barney can hear.

My body reacts by drawing in a huge breath.

A warm palm slips across my mouth.

Ryder's arms curl around my body and my feet leave the floor. He carries me out to the main room and sets me down. His arms stay wrapped around me until I'm steady enough that I won't just topple right over.

"We didn't see that." His voice is low in my ear.

I choke a little, words strangling in my throat. "Okay."

"Just breathe." Ryder stands and rubs my arms up and down. My back is pressed into him, so I can't see his face, but I can feel his chest rising and falling in hitching breaths. "Just breathe and act normal, Marci. We didn't see anything."

Then my phone trills from the bedroom.

"Oh. Shit."

CHAPTER TWO

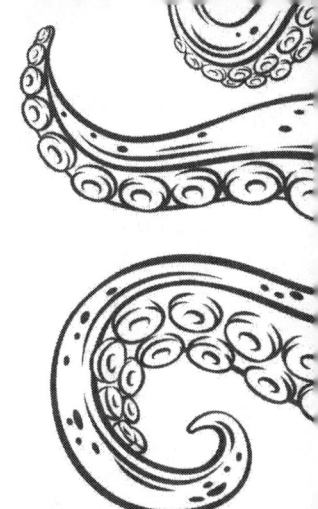

THE BODYGUARD

IN THE WORLD of personal protection officers, the lines of physical professionalism are thin but very firm. The whole point of the job is to be a solid barrier between my subject and the rest of the world. It requires a great sense of trust, understanding, and cooperation.

I've been with Barney Myles for the past four years. Ever since he hit his first number one on the charts and the fans got to be too much. Marci joined the team at the beginning, two years before that.

It was at her urging that I bring my team on for full-time security.

Over the past few years, the three of us have developed a natural rhythm together. We move through the crowds as a fluid unit, and I'm the shield. Marci's the closest to Barney, of course, there to anticipate all of his needs. My job is to watch and anticipate the rest of the world.

But, I never could have anticipated this.

We've both seen Barney in various states of undress.

Between the frantic costume changes backstage at concerts, and then afterward when he comes off for the night sweating and peeling off his shirt in an exhausted slump. Then, there are early mornings like this, when it's just him and a bathrobe.

I appreciate that he's comfortable around us. That he can let loose and be as much of himself as he can be around anyone. Even without the ironclad legal bindings of an NDA, I respect him enough and I've grown to care about him enough as a person that I would never betray his confidence by sharing anything I've seen in those close private moments with the outside world.

That side of Barney Myles is just for me and Marci to see. It's precious and sacred.

The biggest part of this job is remaining objective. A PPO can't identify outward threats if they're too distracted by inward personal feelings. Which is why it's a really bad idea to get involved on an intimate level with one's subject.

Those hard lines that I instilled at the beginning have only smudged softer with time. More recently, they've dissolved into nothing but a blur.

I think what I've just seen may have eviscerated them entirely.

"We need to breathe." I tell Marci, but mostly I'm telling myself. I let her loose and get a little distance between our bodies. I shouldn't like the way her supple curves feel pressed up against me like that.

I shouldn't like the way Barney's wet, slick body looked in that tub, or the way those *tentacles* swayed and curled in the air so thick and glistening.

Marci's phone rings and we both jump. In two long strides, I dash into the bedroom and snatch it up. Careful to keep low and close to the wall in case Barney hears.

I return to the main room where Marci's pacing and offer the phone. "It's your mom."

"She's gonna have to chill her tits." She snatches it out of my grasp and silences the call.

"Yeah." I run my hand over my closely cropped hair. My stomach hollows out and fills with a million questions buzzing around just below my sternum.

She taps out a quick message with shaking thumbs and tosses the phone onto the couch. "What are we going to do?"

"Nothing." I keep my voice just above a whisper. "We're not going to do a fucking thing."

"But—" She glances up to me, green eyes shining and watery. Crimson freckles pop brightly across the canvas of her starkly pale skin. Her wild curls fan out in wisps framing her round face. She threw on her glasses this morning, not bothering with contacts yet. "How could he not tell us? All this time. Fuck. How did we miss... *that*?"

"I don't know." I shake my head and clench my jaw. "If he wanted us to know he would have told us. He can't know that we know."

The suite door swings open and Barney is framed by the doorway standing on human legs just as usual. His towel-dried hair is richly brown and still mussed. The hotel robe swallows his lanky frame. That glow of happiness is replaced with a withdrawn edginess and caution that I'd always chalked up to the weariness of world-renowned fame.

He's exactly like I've seen him hundreds of times. Except now I feel as though I've never seen him before in my life. My heart clinches knowing that the happiness and freedom he'd been feeling moments ago has vanished.

"Morning." His head is down and he shuffles over to the coffee cups on the table. "Ooh, is this from that place I like?"

Marci stills beside me. We're staring.

He peeks up at us cautiously beneath those lush dark eyelashes. An eyebrow arches. "Everything okay?"

"Books 'N Brews." Marci blurts out. I clear my throat and go take a seat in one of the side chairs. "It's from Books N' Brews."

"Yeah! I love this stuff." He folds up on the couch and takes a long slow sip. His eyes shutter and there's a flicker of that bliss again. Almost. It feels like a glimpse of the sun through a rainstorm. "Mm. You didn't have to go out of your way, did you?"

"It's just a few blocks up." Marci finally eases down to her seat.

Barney hugs the cup with both hands. "I can't believe you remembered."

"I know everything about you, Barns." Marci's voice is a little too quiet. A little too heavy. They lock eyes for a moment. I nudge her boot with my toe. She blinks. "It's my job."

"Yeah. I guess it is." The sun vanishes from his face and the clouds sweep in again, dark and thunderous. He stares out the window at the bleak winter sky. "Anyway, thanks."

"It's no big deal." Marci scrolls through her phone. "We've got a pretty straightforward day. Breakfast is on the way up now. In 92 minutes, we depart for rehearsal and sound check at the Garden. After that there's an interview with a local podcast. Then back here for lunch and rest until the concert tonight."

"Cool." Barney nods, but there's no enthusiasm there. He glances over to me and that piercing blue gaze cuts straight into my chest like a lance of sunshine glimmering across clear blue tropical waves. "Think it's gonna be crazy?"

"The venue will be the worst. Fans have been camped out there since last night." I scrub my palms on my jeans. "The studio where we're doing the podcast will have some attention, mostly from papzz. They've been teasing the interview for a week now so it's not a secret you'll be there. But, we're expecting that. There's local security, NYPD, plus my team. Shouldn't be any trouble. Same as usual, you both stick close to me and it'll be fine."

"Got it." Barney's knuckles turn pale as he grips the cup. He chews his bottom lip for a second. "Any chance we'll be going by the big tree?"

"You want to see the Rockefeller Christmas Tree?" Marci lifts her head.

"We've never been around during the Holidays. I was kind of hoping to see it all lit up." Barney shrugs and drops his head. "If it's too much trouble, it's okay. I get it."

"It's kind of a tourist trap." I lean forward and massage the back of my neck while I run through logistics in my mind. A little elf starts tapping a hammer behind my eyes at the mere thought of trying to navigate Christmas Eve crowds. "We'll see."

Marci gives me a pleading look, and I know it's important. He hardly ever asks for anything. If I can give him something like this, I really want to.

"Maybe we can drive by on the way to the concert," Marci adds.

"Yeah. Maybe." Barney deflates. He pushes up off the couch.

"We'll do everything we can to make it happen, Barney," I put all the earnestness into my voice that I can manage, but I still feel like an utter shitbag.

He keeps his head tucked and saunters off into the dressing room with his coffee. "Let me know when breakfast is here."

CHAPTER THREE

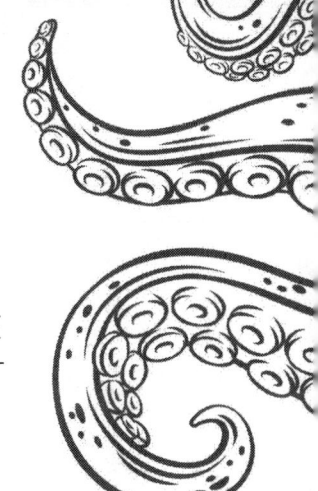

THE ROCKSTAR

SOMETHING'S up with Marci and Ryder.

I've been noticing for a while now. It's the way he watches her when she comes into a room. The way she watches him when he walks out.

The way their eyes gleam when the other speaks.

Today just got weird. Now they're quiet and painted in guilt.

I wonder if they finally hooked up.

I want to be glad for them if it means they're happy. The truth is, thinking about them in each other's arms brings a knot to my throat. An ache so tight in my chest it crushes me from the inside out.

I want something that simply isn't possible.

Then again, I've done so many incredible things I never imagined would be possible. It should all be enough. It feels selfish and greedy to want more.

I gnaw on the string of my hoodie and stare out the darkened window of our nondescript SUV as New York City rolls by. It's supposed to be the place where dreams are made into reality. I've always felt such hope and excitement here.

If I could make one more wish with even the smallest spark of hope, this is the place I know that could make it come true.

My phone buzzes a silent alert in my hand. I glance down to see a message from Marci slide up on my screen.

You ok?

I keep my head down, but glance at her from the corner of my eye. She's right next to me in the seat. She could just ask if she wanted to. Instead, she knocks my thigh with her knee and ducks forward a little so she can peek at my face.

I hold back a smile, but I nudge her with my elbow and text back.

Fine. Focused.

I pull up my hood and scrunch down lower in the seat, putting a sliver of air between us. Not because I want to. Ryder glances back in the mirror he's got lowered on the passenger side while the driver keeps his attention on the creeping traffic surrounding us.

"Five minutes out," he says.

Marci leans forward and scrounges around in her Mary Poppins bag. Everything is in that bag. It's bottomless. Sometimes I think she could yank a blue whale out of it if I asked her to.

Instead, she removes a protein bar and an electrolyte drink that she passes over to me. I take them and eat and drink, but they taste like salty cardboard. My limbs are still heavy from rehearsal, but in a good way. Used, but not exhausted. I was careful not to overdo it.

It's different during a show. Tonight I'll be singing for twenty-thousand screaming fans.

Their energy fuels me. I sing for them and they fill me right back up.

It's pure magic.

But during rehearsals, it's only the crew and my dancers and backup singers.

It drains me.

Ryder's phone rings and he answers it. "Yeah? Shit. How's the side entrance looking?"

I perk up and listen in, but try not to be too obvious about it. Up ahead the sidewalk is getting crowded with people and they're coming to a standstill.

It's easy to recognize the signs of a mob.

I love my fans, I really do. They're amazing and supportive, and their enthusiasm drives me to keep doing what I love best. All they want is one glimpse of me. A smile and a wave could make their entire life.

At the same time, their adoration is incredibly isolating. I can't go anywhere without meticulous planning. To be recognized means getting swamped. It means creating problems for the business owners of the places I might try to visit.

So, I've come to exist solely within hotel rooms and darkly tinted SUVs, with the occasional foray out onto a stage where I soak up my songs echoed back to me by thousands of screaming fans.

I wonder if they'd still feel the same way about me if they knew my secret. Or would their screams of adoration turn into screams of horror?

There's no time to let my mind swim up that river.

Instead, the SUV pulls up to a stop and Ryder turns around to face us. There's an identical vehicle behind us with the rest of the primary security team. They open the doors and pile out while Ryder runs down the order we're going in.

Then he's out and Marci's squeezing my hand. "Hey, you good?"

"Yeah." I cling to her and then the door is open and the muffled roar turns into a deafening ringing.

"Head down. Watch your feet." Ryder's hand lands on my back at the base of my neck as I step out. The pitch turns from deafening to super sonic. NYPD officers hold back the crowd behind barriers with just enough space to keep the alley clear so we can rush through.

Eager hands grab and tug at me and Ryder slips his body in between me and the barriers on the closest side. I keep a tight grip on Marci's hand. We follow after Ken, while Ryder stays on my left side. Carlos is on my right. Somewhere bringing up the back behind Marci is Theo.

My hoodie is up and my head is down.

I block out the flashes and the clawing hands and the screams. It's like a storm out in the deep sea. Nothing but chaos. The screams lodge deep within my chest and steal my breath away. I feel like I'm drowning.

A few paces into the narrow alley, and it already grows quieter. Then a door swings open and there's another guard in uniform and we dash into a low-ceilinged hallway lined with peach painted cinder blocks.

I glance around and account for everyone. It looks like we all just came through a cyclone.

"Everyone got all their limbs?" Ryder checks.

We all give loose nods and I let go of Marci's hand.

"This way, Mr. Myles." An intern in khakis and a white button up with a badge around his neck holds the elevator open.

"Thanks, pal. Good to see you," I tell him. My nod lights up his face with a grin so huge it looks like it might crack his skull.

I step into the tiny elevator and plant my back against the shiny stainless-steel wall.

Another building, another elevator.

I can honestly say I have no idea where in the world I even am. Marci steps in and Ryder's bulk takes up what's left of the space. Outside, the rest of the team waits for the next one.

"24th floor," the intern tells Ryder.

He punches the button and the doors close.

I release a sigh of relief and catch Marci staring at my feet. Ryder's got a weird look on his face too. "What's with you guys today? Why are you acting so weird?"

"Weird?" Marci scoffs. "Your face is weird."

I glance over at Ryder who flushes a deep shade of rose-gold. He mutters, "Marce, what the fuck?"

"Sorry. Reflex. I used to say that to my brothers. Your face is fine, Barns. It's great. Perfect, actually," Marci rushes in. "It's a podcast anyway, nobody's going to be looking at your face."

I would have brushed it off as the joke I know she meant for it to be, but now her neck and cheeks are glowing neon pink and I'm even more suspicious.

"Yeah, okay." I cut her off to save us all the awkwardness of an apology. "Forget it."

The elevator slows and stops. I run my hand through my hair and brush my hood off, ready to turn on my charm for whoever I'm about to spend an hour chatting with, but I don't miss the palpable look that passes between Marci and Ryder as I pass between them.

Yeah. Something is definitely up with these two.

CHAPTER FOUR
THE MANAGER

"YOUR FACE IS WEIRD?" Ryder mocks me. "What are you, twelve?"

"Shut up." I whisper-shout, and slap him across the stomach. It's like backhanding a brick wall. We're in the sound booth looking out to the studio where Barney sits across from the interviewer.

His charm is turned up to eleven and he's joking around in that adorably charismatic way he does that makes everybody instantly love him. It even worked on me at first, and I had a huge crush that I kept to myself for obvious professional reasons.

Now I'm still smitten, and love him, but in a way that's filled with mutual respect and admiration. A way that comes from seeing exactly how much work he puts into his music. The quiet moments when he struggles to find just the right lyric, and the sigh he finally releases in the car after a show.

There's a vulnerability there that I feel a deep desire to protect. I catch it now, in the way he fidgets with his hoodie string. To anyone else, he's just playing. To me, it's clear he wants to shove it in his mouth and gnaw on it, and that makes me concerned that he's anxious.

"Something's up with him. I mean, besides... *you know*." I lean in close to Ryder, keeping my voice hushed, and he ducks his head down to mine. The guy in the sound booth has his headphones on, monitoring the conversation he's recording. I don't think he can hear us, but I'd rather not take any chances.

"It's a show day." Ryder's breath tickles my face. His mouth is so close, so full. I get a little dizzy. "He always gets antsy."

"I know, but—" Right then, Barney glances over.

I'm not sure if the lights in the studio are dim enough for him to see us, but I feel his gaze like he's just cracked open my rib cage and he can see straight inside my chest. The corners of his eyes tighten a little and something hollow crosses his face for a split second before he's back to nodding and answering the last question the interviewer lobbed at him.

I frown. "Do you think he knows we know?"

"I don't know." Ryder straightens and continues our whisper chat. "But he already thinks we're acting weird. He knows *something*. Not to mention the pressure of keeping a thing like that under wraps. It's got to be exhausting."

The door to the booth opens and Barney's business manager, Rick Hartwell, enters. He's sleek and polished, with perfectly clipped salt-and-pepper hair, but somehow still casual in a black knit half-zip pullover and dark jeans with cognac Chelsea boots.

"Marci. Ryder." We all shake hands and turn back to watch Barney. "How's our boy?"

"Good. Fine." I respond a little too quickly.

Hartwell turns an astute assessment onto me for a second. Does *he* know about the tentacles?

Fuck, Marci. Get it together.

"He's great. Really." I shrug, trying to play it off. "It's just the end of the tour. Three continents. Six countries. Eight weeks. I think he's ready for a break."

"Hmm." Heartwell only flattens his lips together. "It's been a whirlwind for us all. We've just got this last stretch of the UK press junket until New Year's. I'll see what I can do about working in a cushion before we get him back in the studio. I don't think it would be an issue to push back recording until February, if he wants to."

"That'd be good." I keep an eye on Barney. The interview is about to wrap up. Then I remember. "Is there anything we can do about getting him over to see the Christmas tree?"

"At Rockefeller? Today?" Hartwell acts like I'm the one who just sprouted tentacles. "Jesus. It's a fucking madhouse over there. Wall-to-wall."

"I know. I get it. He's just never seen it, and it's the one thing he asked for." My chest tightens. "I was wondering if maybe you knew a place we could slip in somewhere that might have a view."

"Ah, yeah." Hartwell checks a message on his smartwatch. "Sure. I'll see what I can put together."

The interview is over and Barney's removing his headphones. He gives a fistbump to the host and we head out to the hallway to meet them. Everyone gathers and greetings are exchanged while I slip Barney a fresh bottle of his favorite water and a honey lozenge.

The host is clearly smitten with Barney. I honestly don't know anyone who's met him that hasn't been. He's magnetic. But as his personal manager, I also can't help but feel a little territorial.

Everyone assumes they know him because they keep up with him online. They get the occasional social media posts, thinking it's a close glimpse into his personal life. Except, those are highly curated and run through PR first. Barney's never even seen his social media accounts.

Speaking of which...

"Everybody get in, let's get a shot for the 'gram." I shoo Barney, the host, and Hartwell in together and snap a few pictures while they pose. Then I check to make sure no one has their eyes closed and text a few of the best ones over to his publicist Mikayla to post on his account. "Got it, thanks."

The host heads back inside the studio and we move in a pod toward the elevator. Hartwell scoops an arm around Barney's shoulders and sags a little. "Soo. I've got some news."

Barney slows his steps and braces himself. I clench my fists wondering what the fuck is going on and how Rick could be enough of a douche to break some kind of bad news a few hours before a concert.

Hartwell holds up his hand. "How many fingers am I holding up?"

"Two." Barney glances between Hartwell's fingers and his face. Then tosses a desperate look to me like I might know what the fuck is going on.

"That's right. You've just gone multi-platinum!" Hartwell breaks out into a huge grin. Relief washes through me so fast my knees gel. Ryder's there with a touch to the small of my back to keep me upright.

"Oh, my god." My jaw drops and I let out a bubble of laughter. "Barney!"

I think if Rick didn't already have a good hold on Barney's shoulders he'd melt into a puddle right there on the floor. His eyes light up in a bright sparkle as he processes the news.

"Wow." A flush creeps up his neck and he swallows twice and shakes his head. Rick grabs him and pulls him into a rough hug.

Then Barney's arms are around my neck. He's taller than me, but not by a whole lot. His body is thin and lanky, all sinewy dancer's muscles and he smells like bubble bath and something I'd never been able to put my finger on before.

The ocean.

His fingertips squeeze my back and I flash to those suckers on the window and can't help but tuck my nose up against his neck for just a second. His freshly shaven cheek is still soft as I press a quick kiss to his jaw. I hold his face in my hands and our eyes lock for just a second and I want so much to let him know that I *see* him.

"Congratulations," I tell him instead.

His gaze dips down to my lips for a mere fraction of a second. "Thanks."

Then Ryder tugs my shirt and I let my hands drop and then they're doing that handshake bro-hug thing with a high five and a snap.

"Celebration lunch?" Hartwell asks. "I got us a spot at Nobu."

Barney's excited flush drains in an instant.

"No!" I can't stop my shout.

Hartwell casts a strange look at me.

"No sushi," I say. Barney's eyes narrow and he goes completely still. "He's allergic to shellfish."

"Since when?" Hartwell cants his head.

Barney drives a hand through his tousled hair and plays it off, but now he refuses to look at me. "Since always, man."

"How about Carmine's?" Ryder suggests. "It's not far, and I know the manager. They've got a discreet entrance and some good seating out of the way upstairs."

"Yeah, okay I could go for some pasta." Rick grabs Barney again in a rough hug and jabs the button for the elevator. "Let's do it."

Ryder gives me a hard *what the fuck* look over both their heads while we wait for the elevator. We all cram in and make it downstairs, then hold tight and make small-talk about the final leg of the tour while Ryder gets the new plans squared away with the rest of the team and the restaurant.

Hartwell practically attaches himself to Barney at the hip. All I want to do is have a minute alone with him, but that's clearly not going to be possible. He still won't look at me and his jaw keeps ticking in the corner. He's smaller and hunched down inside his hoodie and it feels like he's standing right in the center of my chest.

Fuck.

Ryder gives us the all-clear and we're back out

through the gauntlet of fans and press. It's just a few blocks up to the restaurant, but Hartwell rides in the car with us so I take the back seat since technically he's my boss and he gets priority.

I check the time and calculate how long lunch will be.

All I can think about is Barney's face when he asked about seeing the Christmas tree. How could one simple thing be so difficult? I glance out into Times' Square at all the tourists taking selfies and a leisurely stroll to see the sights.

I hate that Barney can't be one of them. If he showed up here it'd be absolute chaos. We pass by a cart with a guy selling some unique merchandise that catches my eye. I press my hand to the window and peer out trying to get a better look.

My breath catches.

Suddenly I feel like the Grinch and an evil grin spreads across my face as I get a wonderful, awful idea.

CHAPTER FIVE

THE BODYGUARD

"NO." My stomach bottoms out and I take a stance, towering over Marci in the hallway by the restrooms. "Absolutely fucking not. We're not doing that. No fucking way."

She juts out her lower lip and it's so goddamned kissable I nearly pass out from the sudden blood loss to my brain. "He needs this. Please. It's a brilliant idea."

"It's a terrible idea." It's a *genius* idea and I'm honestly kinda pissed I didn't think of it myself. "We could get fired for trying to pull something like this."

"Only if we get caught." She bats her long lashes and looks so cute I can't stand it. "And we aren't going to get caught."

I cross my arms over my chest and pull myself up to my full height. "Don't look at me like that. I'm impervious to all puppy-dog pouts."

"You know you want to." She dangles a ridiculous knit hat in front of me. I shift on the balls of my feet and try to hold out but then I remember the look on Barney's face this morning and I know how much this really would mean to him.

She's not wrong.

He *does* deserve this.

"Fine." I cave. "Don't make me regret this."

CHAPTER SIX

THE ROCKSTAR

I TAP my heel against my chair leg. It's too hard to sit still.

What the hell did Marci mean, I'm allergic to shellfish? I've never said anything to her, never so much as hinted at what I really am. Maybe she just saw me get a little queasy at the thought of my tentacles being hacked to bits by a cleaver.

I want to ask her what she knows, but if it's not that, I can't give myself away. I've been so careful. Nobody knows. *Nobody*.

All I can do is pick at my pasta and watch Rick down another glass of wine.

I can't even have any. With a show tonight, I need to stay hydrated. The news about my latest album going platinum again is phenomenal. It's so great, I want to be thrilled and I am. At the same time, I'm also terrified that I did something or said something, that I slipped up.

Marci excused herself from the table almost fifteen

minutes ago, and then Ryder slipped out. They've been gone another five minutes.

Are they hooking up in the bathroom?

The thought of them together shouldn't fill me with this kind of dread. It shouldn't fill me with anything but happiness.

It's a good thing when two people find love. But I can't quell that swimming feeling I get deep down in my stomach when I think of them together. I grip the edge of the table and swallow a moan. If only I could get to the Christmas tree and make my wish....

I gnaw the inside of my lip and try to hold back the emotion that's rushing up.

Rick gets his card back from the server and stands up.

"I hate to eat and run but I've got to get down to the Garden. Get some rest." He gives me a fist bump. "I'll see you tonight, buddy."

"Later." He heads out and I'm sitting here alone.

That heavy weight of loneliness settles deep in the middle of my chest. It feels like I'm trying to swallow past a rock. My thoughts trip and skip over one another too fast to latch onto. It sounds like a radio trying to be tuned too fast to catch a station.

I hate being alone. As loud and wild as the fans get, at least I know I'm not alone when they're there.

We're in a private room and I duck out. Theo's there and I nod to him. He trails behind me to the restrooms and I find Ryder and Marci right outside in what appears to be some kind of standoff.

Then she jumps up and down and lets out an

obscene dolphin squeal that jolts straight through my body.

"Go ahead." Ryder motions to me. "Tell him your genius plan."

I stop short. "What plan?"

Marci peers around me. "Where's Hartwell?"

"He had to go," I say.

"Perfect!" Marci holds up a weird knitted thing that looks like it has a shaggy brown mop attached. "Put this on."

"What is it?" I turn the thing around and discover that it's a knitted hat with a beard attached.

The hat part is silver with white horns sticking out of the top like a Viking helmet. The yarn that makes up the beard hangs down long and loose with two braids dangling from a mustache.

I glance between them. "Why am I putting this on?"

"It's a disguise, you goob!" Marci takes another one out of the bag and yanks it down over her curls. It's a big green trapper hat with faux fur and a shaggy black beard that covers half her face and all of her bright red hair.

Aside from her distinctive freckles, I don't even recognize her with it on. Understanding dawns on me and a ray of hope shrinks the stone in my chest.

She grabs another hat for Ryder and shoves it in his hands. "This one's for you."

He takes one look at it. "No fucking way. He can wear this one."

"The whole point is so he doesn't get attention. If everybody's looking at you they won't be looking at him." She's small but mighty.

And she's brilliant.

Ryder gives me a desperate look and I shrug, barely able to contain my laugh. "She's not wrong."

"You both are gonna owe me so big for this." He puts on the bright red cap with a big white pom on top, and a fluffy white yarn beard. His shoulders sag in defeat.

"Hey, Santa. Do I get to sit on your lap and tell you what I want for Christmas?" Theo laughs so hard he doubles over. "Marci, you're a genius."

"Yeah, yeah." Ryder sighs. "Laugh it up, knuckleheads."

"How do I look?" I put my own hat on and Marci beams.

"Perfect." She hands us some cheap plastic sunglasses. "These too. And take off your hoodie."

A couple of the service staff are standing by grinning like goofballs. I'm sure Ryder's already hit them with NDAs and probably confiscated their cell phones until we leave so they can't sneak any photos.

We borrow their heavy winter coats and the disguise is complete.

"Theo." Ryder points to him. "You guys good?"

He wipes away a tear and waves at us. "It's fine, boss. Go. Have fun."

"Where *are* we going?" I fall into step behind Ryder and he leads us down a long, nondescript hallway. A few turns later and we come out in a back alley.

There's a white delivery truck waiting with exhaust curling a wispy cloud in the frigid air.

"Hang on." I skid to a stop. Marci bumps into my back. The weirdness that's been going on today makes more sense. A wave of panic crashes through me. "Are you guys abducting me?"

"Oh my god, Barney." Marci rolls her eyes and Ryder picks her up and places her in the back of the truck. "We're springing you loose. Consider it more like a prison break."

Ryder turns to me. "We've got three hours. Wanna play tourist?"

I stand there and gape at them, shaking my head a little in astonishment. This is almost too good to be true.

Marci and Ryder all to myself for the rest of the afternoon?

"Yes. Please. Let's do this."

CHAPTER SEVEN

THE BODYGUARD

NORMALLY, I'd like a little more planning than this. No, a *lot* more. It takes an enormous amount of logistics and coordination to keep Barney safe.

But here we are, in the back of a non-descript delivery truck, heading out into the concrete jungle. If anything happens to the world's most famous rockstar, the number one prize of Gold Needle Records, the label won't just fire me... they'll end my life as I know it.

No pressure.

I grip my thighs as we bounce and jolt like milk bottles crammed in between boxes of meat and produce.

This is fine.

We're completely in the hands of Fate and our driver Giulio. There are already about a thousand things that could go wrong, and it's literally my job to think of all of them and prepare a solution for how to deal with them *just in case*.

"Relax." Marci jabs an elbow into my ribs. She turns

her face up to me, but Barney's gone still. He's facing a box with the word CALAMARI printed on the side.

Shit.

I jerk my chin and she turns around. "Oh! Hey, uh Barns, what do you want to do first?"

He snaps out of his trance and his eyes flick between us. "Uh, hell. I don't know."

"The world is your oyster!"

I knee Marci in the ass at the same time the truck lurches to a stop I brace as she and Barney smash up against me. I keep my long arm around both of them until we regain our balance.

"I mean, uhm... you wanted to see the tree. Anything else?" She keeps her tone light.

Barney looks up at me and his face is unreadable. His eyes go soft and darken within the midst of his disguise and my balls twinge.

The back door slides up and we're hit with the murky daylight again and the spell is over.

"Here we are, Rockefeller Plaza!" Giulio announces.

I hop out first and then help out Barney and Marci. Marci slips Giulio some cash and a wink. I don't know how much she's handed over in this little endeavor already but I'm positive it's a ridiculous amount.

I'm also positive every cent is completely worth it when Giulio pulls away and I see the look of wonder shining on Barney's face.

CHAPTER EIGHT
THE ROCKSTAR

"NOBODY'S SCREAMING." I hold still and glance around. "Nobody's even looking at me. What is this madness?"

"See? I told you!" Marci giggles and bounces up and down, clapping her hands. The few people jostling past us glance over at Ryder because he's dressed like Santa. The plan is working perfectly. It's like I don't even exist.

This is amazing.

"Yeah, okay." Ryder's yarn-beard twitches and he scoops us into motion, one heavy, muscular arm around each of us. "Let's get moving before they catch on."

I'm so used to looking out at the people, but not being with them. It's exhilarating. We're swept along like a flash flood in a flowing current of rushing bodies.

Up ahead there's a tighter knot off to one side and Ryder steers us over. He's almost a head taller than everyone else and it's nice being pressed up against his hard body.

I feel safe and comfortable here.

Then I recognize an angel statue alight with a sparkling trumpet and my heart stutters. The other tourists take a few selfies and then move aside and it's just *there*.

My mouth drops open, and Ryder's arm tightens around me. I sink against him and my vision blurs.

"Whoa."

It doesn't even feel real. I've only ever seen the giant Christmas tree on screen in movies and TV, and in photos. But now it's right there and it's glowing and filling my heart up so full it starts leaking out my eyes before I can stop it.

Then Marci's arms curl around my waist and I throw my arm over her shoulders. Ryder encloses us both in his enormous embrace.

"Everything you hoped it would be?" His voice is low and soft in my ear.

I swallow hard. "Yeah. It is."

I tilt my head and Marci leans in until we're propped up together. I'm annoyed the hats are in the way. I only want more of her face next to mine, like back in the hallway when my heart stopped completely the moment she brushed her lips against my cheek.

I hold them both tighter and stare up at the sparkling star on top of the tree. I gather up everything I want and send my wish out to the Fates above and below. Warmth gathers at my center and I know I've done all I can do.

"Thanks, Marce." My voice is choked with emotion.

"You're welcome." She squeezes me. "Wanna see it up close?"

I nod. "But first...."

I take out my phone and grab a few photos. Then we scrunch in together and Ryder takes a selfie because he has the longest arms.

"Hey, did you want us to take a picture of you?" A tourist steps up, and I freeze. Ryder eases up in front of me, and Marci crowds against my side, curling her hand around my arm. "Then you take one of us?"

"Sure." My heart thuds. "Great idea."

"Your hats are really hilarious," she says.

"Thanks. They're super warm," Marci tells her.

I hand over my phone and we pose again. She takes a few shots and then hands them back for me to check. My heart is thrumming and my fingers are numb but I manage a smile. "Thanks."

I take her phone and she lines up with her friends.

"Say jingle bells!" I tell them.

They all laugh and shout and I snap away.

"Thank you so much!" She takes her phone back.

I wave. "Happy holidays."

They head off into the crowd grinning and chatting with each other.

I glance over at Ryder and Marci and we collapse in on each other in a pile of stupid, hysterical laughter.

I can hardly believe it.

My wish is already starting to come true and it's the absolute best.

CHAPTER NINE

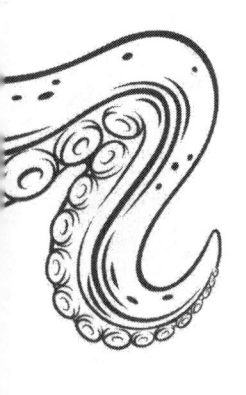

THE MANAGER

BARNEY'S like a little kid and I can't take my eyes off him. I hadn't realized how accustomed I'd become to his quiet, withdrawn nature. It makes me worry how deeply the fame and notoriety has been affecting him. It's my job to notice these things and I feel sick that it took me so long to realize it for what it was.

Now there's a light in his eyes I haven't seen in such a long time.

It ignites something in my chest and I feel hot and full and weightless like a hot air balloon.

Ryder uses his bulk to part the crowd, and Barney holds his hand as he trails behind. I follow, clasping Barney's other hand, and it's the longest we've probably ever had solid skin-to-skin contact.

There's nothing to worry about, though. Right now, we're not work colleagues, or a rockstar and his manager. We're just two friends enjoying the holiday sights.

Warmth seeps up my arm, crawling like a live vine straight into my chest. It pours down through my belly and settles low, filling me up with something more than mere arousal. I'm not sure I've ever experienced this kind of need before.

It's unsettling and I like it.

We make it as close as we can to the tree and we stand there together in a little tripod with Barney in the middle. The crowd moves around us and I don't even notice them. It's just us and the tree, and I feel something solid click into place.

I take a chance and slip my arm around Barney and he snuggles against me. He wiggles his hips and Ryder closes his hand around my arm, squeezing us both.

Barney sighs and there are no words.

It's perfect.

We gaze up at the lights for who knows how long, and finally Barney loosens his grip and we break our embrace, but stick close to each other. He drags us over to glance down at the ice rink.

I watch his face, and I've already got my phone out looking up ticket options when he asks, "Can we go skating?"

"No. No way." Ryder shakes his head so hard I'm worried it'll fall off his shoulders. "I'm not gonna have you break a leg right before a show."

I wince. He does make a good point.

"Ryderrr." Barney literally whines and throws himself up against his bodyguard. "You played hockey, didn't you?"

"I—" Ryder blinks. "Yeah. How'd you remember that?"

"Doesn't matter." Barney grabs him and he's already

dragging us toward the rink. "You're good at skating and you're my bodyguard. I can't break a leg if you're there to protect me."

I trail after them and exchange a glance with Ryder. Also, a very good point.

"Yeah, well, the line is probably too long anyway," Ryder says. "We only have so much time before we have to get you over to the show."

A few clicks on my phone and all three of us have season passes. Members don't have to schedule a time, we can just go. It's the best $1,650 I've ever spent.

Ryder's eye roll when we zoom past the line to get our skate rental is the cherry on top. I'm no expert by any means, but I had enough lessons back when I was going through my Tara Lipinski phase as a kid that the technique comes back to me after a few shaky seconds.

Like riding a bike.

Ryder's clearly the most comfortable out of all of us, and he skates backward holding Barney's hands while he instructs him on the basics.

I stay close behind, ready to... what? I have no idea. Throw my body down as a pillow, I guess.

Now, I'm suddenly terrified of more than just a broken limb. If Barney falls, he could get a concussion, or worse. People zoom past us and it's unnerving.

Then Barney laughs as he gets the hang of it. Ryder grins. And fuck it all, this is *fun*.

"You're a natural." Ryder lets go of one of Barney's hands and moves in beside him. I skate up and take the other.

"This is so cool!" Barney's grin is contagious.

We go around in a leisurely circle, gaining confidence with each lap. It's magical with the tree overhead, and snow even begins to fall and grow heavier within a few minutes.

Barney tilts his head back a little and Ryder and I steady him between us. He's not skating so much as he's just standing between us while we drag him along. But, he looks so peaceful and free.

I never imagined this could be anything I ever wanted, but it's magical and it's perfect. We sweep around the rink and I glance up at the star on the tree. If I could wish for anything for Christmas, it would be for this feeling to never end.

CHAPTER TEN

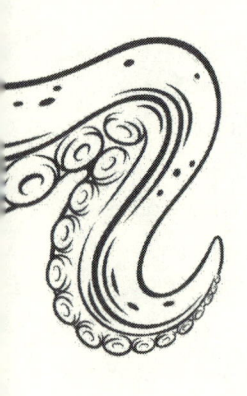

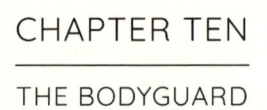

THE BODYGUARD

WE'RE out on the ice for almost an hour before I call it. The temperature is dropping exponentially. Even though our heads and bodies are warm inside our jackets and hats, our hands and noses are still exposed.

Not to mention, the cold air can't be good for Barney's voice.

I glance up to the observation deck and nod to Theo. The rest of the crew is positioned in strategic spots, and I don't think Barney has noticed. His life is in my hands, I'm not going to be completely irresponsible with it.

"Hey, one more lap." I break the news to Barney. "Then we need to head in."

"Two more?" he pleads.

"Ugh. Fine." I'm such a pushover, but two won't make a difference at this point. "I can't say no to you."

"Because I'm so adorable?" He flashes his impeccable teeth at me and there's snow catching in that ridiculous yarn beard.

Marci snorts out a laugh.

I can't admit the truth. That here on this rink with a giant glowing Christmas tree overhead, and the snow falling around us in big fluffy chunks, he's completely irresistible.

"Yeah." I roll my eyes and play it off. "Don't let it go to your head."

"You think I'm cuuute," he sings and the snow catches in his eyelashes. "You think I'm seeexy. You wanna—waghh!"

He leans forward a little too much and trips up. I swing forward and he tumbles into my arms. I have us balanced until Marci collides with him, and then we all go down in one big heap.

I take the brunt of the fall, catching Barney between my legs. Marci lands on top and rolls down against his side. I manage to keep my head from hitting the ice and we slide a few feet before coming to a halt.

They're both staring up at me in stunned silence. I've got their weight between my thighs and holy shit, it feels good. I gulp down a breath as we lay there with puffs of white gathering around our heads.

"Toepick," I mutter.

Marci drops her head and starts shaking. It takes a second before she looks up again and howls out a laugh. Barney lets out a huff and starts up, too. I want to join them, but my heart is pounding up in my throat and I can't manage a sound.

The tree is shimmering above us through the falling snow. The star at the top twinkles in the growing darkness.

This.

This right here is what I want with my whole heart. If I could have any wish come true, it would be this. Forever.

Luckily we're close to the railing, so Marci drags herself up first, then helps Barney. They both try to haul me up, but nearly fall again and I wave them away and get up to brush myself off.

We're soaked and cold and tired, and it's absolutely perfect.

"Come on, you goobs." I steer them over to the exit. "Let's get inside."

We trade in our skates and Marci veers off to get us some hot chocolate. There's an empty spot off to the side by a stairwell, so I lead Barney over. Before I peel off his hat, I angle him into the corner away from the security cameras in the main hall and any passers by that might catch a glimpse.

His nose is bright as a Maraschino cherry, and his fingers are like icicles, but his eyes are crisp and clear and dancing. "You good?"

"Yeah. That was so fun." A shiver runs through him as I take his hands, trying to rub some warmth back in. "This is the best, Ryder. Seriously."

"As long as you don't have frostbite." I take off my hat and bring his hands to my mouth, then blow warm air over them.

His lips part and his breath hitches.

"These are incredibly talented hands." I press his fingers up against my cheeks. "Can't have your fingers falling off."

"Yeah, that'd be bad." He stares at the spot where his

palm presses against my mouth. A buzz sets up in the base of my spine, and it's definitely not aftershocks from the fall.

His fingers go still and I press my lips into a lingering kiss.

I've seen up close what these hands can do, moving across a keyboard and along the neck of a guitar with grace and precision. There's a reason he's a multi-platinum musician and it isn't his gorgeous face. Although, that doesn't really hurt.

"I don't think that's working," he whispers.

"No?" I arch a brow and pause, not sure if he wants me to stop or... *ohh*.

He moves his hands down and slides them up under my shirt. I gasp and jam my back up against the wall with the shock of the cold on my heated abs. It steals my breath at first, and then I ease into his touch.

"Is this okay?" he asks softly.

I try to say it's probably not very professional, but the only thing that comes out of my mouth is, "Don't stop."

His fingertips prod along my muscled abs and trace the curves upward. My nipples peak and rub against my shirt. I can't stop the quiet grunt that rises up in the back of my throat. Barney leans into me and my hips jut forward to meet his.

"Your nose looks cold, too." I reach up and feather the back of my knuckle down the perfectly sculpted bridge of his nose, and his eyelashes flutter shut.

He lets out a peaceful sigh and I repeat the motion.

"What are you guys *doing*?" Marci hisses at us.

We jerk apart and a heated flush creeps up my neck

into my face. I'm glad the coat I borrowed is long enough because I have a suddenly raging hard-on. "I uh...."

"Put your hats back on, you doofs!" Marci smacks me in the face with my hat. "Somebody could recognize you, for fuck's sake."

"Right." It's hard to catch my breath. The hat and beard are stifling now, but I leave them on while Marci helps Barney with his.

I take the moment while they're focused on each other to adjust my jeans and try to stop thinking about those slick wet tentacles from this morning.

Was that seriously only a few hours ago? It feels like a lifetime.

Shit, we still haven't mentioned it. But we can't, not at least until after the show. He's so happy right now. I don't want to fuck with his focus.

Marci hands out the hot chocolate and checks her phone. "Theo's going to meet us over by the Rainbow Room entrance. ETA, three minutes."

"Back to reality, huh." I notice Barney's a little hunched over as well. "It was good while it lasted. This was seriously the best Christmas present ever, you guys. For real."

His gaze lingers on mine and that lightning strikes up my spine again. Then he grabs Marci's hand and tucks it up under his beard and kisses it.

"It was our pleasure. Really," Marci gets a little wobbly.

Barney weaves his fingers with hers and doesn't let go as they turn and head around for the staircase. He throws a heated glance at me over his shoulder. I stay a step behind until my arousal dies down and we make it up through the maze of the building to find Theo and the rest of the team waiting for us at the curb.

We pile into the heated safety of the SUV and tear off our hats.

Theo shuts us in and takes the front passenger side while I slip into the back seat behind Barney and Marci. A coil of relief unravels in my stomach and I sink down in the seat.

We slip out into traffic and the colorful lights blur and blend with the snow. I can't believe we pulled it off, but we fucking did it.

Miracles happen.

CHAPTER ELEVEN

THE ROCKSTAR

CAREFUL WHAT YOU WISH FOR.

It's a show night and I should be focused on my music, but on the final run throughs, I miss choreography, and I'm late on intros. I end up skipping a whole verse in "Lately I Been Thinking of You," because I'm thinking of Ryder's lips on my palm, and Marci's nose burrowed into my hair on the drive over here.

"Sorry, everyone," I apologize to the band and back-up singers. "Can we go again from the top?"

The drummer counts us off and somehow I manage to make it through. I call it after that and Rick's waiting for me off-stage.

"Everything okay, man?" He whacks my back. "You seem distracted."

Ryder's right there with his thick arms folded across his thick chest. I have to walk past him like I don't even notice, even though my body heats and my insides feel mushy.

I realize Rick is waiting for an explanation. "Nah, those people coming tonight are taking time out away from their families to be here on a holiday. I'm basically their Christmas wish, right? I've got this. They deserve a great show and that's what I'm going to give them."

Rick relaxes.

"Awesome. Glad to hear it. You're going to be amazing." He whacks my arm again. "We're in the home stretch. Last full show tonight, then press in London next week, and a couple of songs for New Year's. I've already talked with Marci and we've got you cleared for all of January. If you need more space before we head back into the studio, just say the word. We'll make it happen."

"I appreciate that. And all of this." I wave my hand to the stage and the rest of the arena. "It's a big job putting this all together."

"You make it easy." Rick grins. "Have a great show."

"Okay." I pause before we part ways. "Have you seen Marci?"

"Yeah, she's in the green room fixing you a plate." He heads off and I toss a glance over to Ryder and head to the green room where there are a few tables and chairs set up along with a buffet of hot food and an assortment of drinks.

A few of the crew members are there at a table, but their plates are empty and they're just chatting. They notice me and say hi before they clear out.

Marci turns and sees me. "Oh, hey. I snagged you some tofu. You'll need some protein. How's your throat? The cold didn't mess with it too much, did it?"

I wave Ryder in and he shuts the door so we have the room to ourselves. "It's fine. I just wanted to thank you both again for today. It really meant a lot to me—*you* mean a lot to me."

Marci gapes for a second then sets the plate down on the table and grabs my hand. "You mean a lot to us too, Barns."

Ryder nods. "We're here for you. Whatever you need. We want you to be safe and happy."

I glance between them and their faces are so genuine and earnest. Marci squeezes my hand and I cling to her. My heart thrums and I can feel my pulse in my palm where our skin is touching.

"There's something I've been wanting to share with you both for a while now, and I think today was the first time I really thought it might be possible." I seal my lips together and as much as I want to, I still can't bring myself to say the words out loud.

Marci's cheeks turn fuschia. She tosses a quick glance up to Ryder and he nods. She smiles a little. "It's okay. We kind of... figured it out."

"You know?" I blink. Now it's my turn to blush. "I didn't realize I'd been that obvious."

"You definitely weren't." Ryder shrugs and smiles a little. "I never would have suspected until this morning."

"This morning." My eyebrows dart up even higher. This whole day makes way more sense. "Is *that* why you were acting weird?"

"Weird?" Marci juts out her hip. "I mean, it was kind of a shock, at first. But in more of an unexpected way, not a bad way. I only wish you'd said something sooner."

"I never really thought it'd be something I was into, but I haven't been able to stop thinking about it all day." Ryder's gaze travels down the length of my body and makes me shiver.

"So... you're okay with it?" Relief washes through me. I can hardly believe it's true. Then again, it's exactly what I wished for.

"Of course." Marci hugs my neck. "It's all good. We were going to talk to you after the concert anyway. We just didn't want to distract you before the show."

I laugh a little and wrap my arms around her. She's so soft. She squeezes against me and our bodies melt together.

It's pure bliss.

I reach up and tangle my hands in her lush curls. It's like silk wrapping around my fingers.

"You're the best." My lips touch her ear and her breath catches.

"I know." I can feel her smile against my cheek.

"Marci." I bring my hands up to cup her face and tumble into the depths of her evergreen gaze. Our foreheads touch and our breath mingles. "I just really want to kiss you so bad right now."

She sucks in a little gasp and then her hand curves around the back of my neck and she's lifting her chin. "Would that make you happy?"

We're so close, my lips brush hers when we speak. I groan with the pang of my desire. "So happy."

"Me too." She takes my mouth finally, and she's just as incredible as I'd hoped. Her lips are like plush silk, and she's soft and warm and welcoming.

I reach out my arm and wave around until it hits solid muscle. I keep kissing Marci, slow and easy, while I wrap my fist in Ryder's shirt.

He lets out a rough gush of air, and I break off from Marci. Her eyes are hooded and pooled dark in the center.

We both turn to look up at Ryder. He towers over us, and his solid form is the exact opposite of Marci's supple curves. How could I be so lucky to get the best of both?

"You too." I yank him down. "I want to taste you, too."

"Don't have to tell me twice." His lips slam onto mine. The stubble on his chin is rough, mixing with the firm press of his mouth against mine and it sends arousal stinging straight down to my balls.

Marci's arms are still around my waist and I roll my hips against the crux of her thighs. Her hand cradles the back of my head, supporting me while Ryder devours my mouth.

I tear away and stumble back. We stand there, chests heaving, mouths beestung and wet, skin flushed and hair mussed.

"Okay." I gulp down a few breaths and hold up my hands. "Okay. You guys are both going to need to not touch me again until the show is over tonight. After that... we'll... figure it out."

They both silently agree.

"Good." I take another step back and laugh a little. "Maybe don't even look at me, either."

"Right." Marci tilts her head back to look at the ceiling.

Ryder picks a spot on the carpet. "Got it."

"Super." I head for the door before I change my mind. "I'll see you after the show."

CHAPTER TWELVE

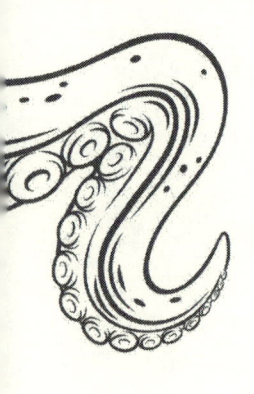

THE MANAGER

THE DOOR CLICKS SHUT and Ryder and I don't move for a second.

I clear my throat. "He wasn't talking about the tentacles."

"Nope." Ryder leans forward and puffs up air in his cheeks.

"Okay." I bounce my head up and down a little. "So we just agreed to—"

"A throuple." Ryder straightens, keeping his eyes on the door.

I shrug. "I was gonna go with ménage, but okay."

"I think two out of three of us have to be married for it to be a ménage à trois." Ryder finally turns to me and scrubs his hand over his short hair. "Throuple implies a more casual arrangement."

All I can do is stare up at him.

He scrunches his nose and it's adorable. "My parents were swingers. I got to know some things."

"Wow." I hide a smile. "Aren't you full of surprises."

"Anyway. I guess it's clear we're both into him." He winds his arms up across his chest and his muscles flex and I go a little cross-eyed. "But what about—"

"Don't even finish that sentence. I've wanted to dick you down since the second I laid eyes on you," I admit.

He lets out a strangled noise and drops his arms. "Really."

Now my heart's pounding again and my throat closes up a little. What if he's just not that into me. "How about you?"

He massages the back of his neck. "Sometimes I hope there's a security breach just so I have an excuse to throw my body on top of yours."

Okay, so he's into me. Rock on.

We both continue standing there. I shift my weight back and forth on the balls of my feet a few times.

"Why does this feel like middle school?" I ask.

"Fuck." He lets out a strong breath. "I have no idea."

I stick my chest out. "Grab my tit."

"Come again?" Ryder's eyes bug.

"That's what she said." I point to my boob. "Grab it. It's okay."

"It's really not sexy when you say it like that." Ryder gazes down at my cleavage. "Shouldn't we maybe kiss or something first?"

"Seriously, you're making it even more awkward." I reach out and take his hand and bring it up until he's hovering right over my chest. "Get a good fistful."

"Marci—"

"For fuck's sake, just grab my tits Ryder!"

He closes his hand on my breast at the same moment

the door to the green room opens and Rick Hartwell walks in.

Ryder swipes at my chest. "Where'd it go?"

"Huh?" Panic freezes me in place.

"Agh!" He stomps on the floor. "Did I get it?"

"I don't know!" I yell.

"Oh, yep." He digs his toe into the carpet and twists a few times. Ryder glances over to Rick. "There was a spider."

"Uh. Right." Rick holds up his phone. "I just wanted to let you know we're keeping a close eye on the weather. A Nor'easter's coming in. They might shut down the airport."

"Will it affect the concert?" I ask.

"No, the subways are still running fine. I expect we'll still be getting a decent crowd." He nods. "We've still got the hotel booked for tonight. We just might have to stay and head across the pond tomorrow."

"Okay. No problem." I smile. "Thanks for the heads up."

"Yep." He glances between us one more time before he slips out.

I sink down in one of the chairs at the table and slap my hand across my forehead. "We're so gonna get fired."

CHAPTER THIRTEEN

THE BODYGUARD

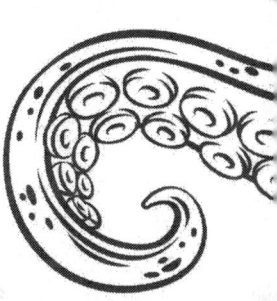

TWENTY-THOUSAND PEOPLE brave a blizzard on Christmas Eve just to see Barney sing and he doesn't let them down. He even does a special encore where he sings a cover of Mariah Carey's "All I Want For Christmas is You."

The fans go so wild, the whole floor vibrates and for a few moments I'm actually making plans for what to do if the roof caves in. They sing and scream along with him while he bops around on stage and it's nothing less than pure magic.

About halfway through, Marci steps up and leans into my side. Her face is bright and happy and there are tears and a big grin smeared all over her face. I give her a perfectly professional side-hug, and we stand there watching the big finale for the last show of the tour.

My heart swells and I have a tough time swallowing past a knot in my throat. It's been an exhausting and fun eight weeks, with a lot of hard work from a lot of people, and Barney's at the center of it all. Sure we get paid well, but honestly I think we'd all want to be here no matter what. Barney is just that charming.

He's got the entirety of Madison Square Garden hanging on every single note. Then the song is over and he remains on stage waving to the crowd as they roar.

He takes his time, soaking it all up before he finally strolls offstage. I realize I still have my arm around Marci, and the hunger in his gaze when he sees us standing there together is overwhelming.

He walks straight into our arms, sweaty and breathless.

Time slows. We capture him in a congratulatory hug and I feel his chest vibrate with a moan meant only for us.

This. This is all I want. We all fit together and it's perfect. This feeling is everything. I'm soaring.

Then time starts again as we break apart and Marci puts an electrolyte gel pack in his hand. Hartwell is there grabbing him into a big handshake and the make-up and wardrobe crew steps in and they're laughing and crying.

The end of a tour is always emotional, but especially tonight. It's Christmas and there's extra magic in the air somehow. Normally, on the last night like this, we'd break everything down and then have a big wrap party for the crew. It's a chance for everyone to celebrate all their hard work, to release and unwind.

Normally, there's not a blizzard raging outside.

Instead, the whole team gathers out on the arena floor and Rick gives a thank you speech. Then, Barney grabs a bottle of champagne and sprays it over everyone from the stage and we all do a toast.

I try my damnedest not to look at Marci and Barney for too long, but it's hard not to stare, especially when they're right next to each other talking with Hartwell.

Before I can be too obvious about it, I grab Theo and we throw on coats and head outside to check the streets.

It's a fucking mess. At least six inches of snow has fallen since we were last outside.

"What do you think, boss?" Theo raises his eyebrows.

I double check the MTA map on my phone and find there's a stop on the same block as the hotel. "I think we're going to have to take the subway."

Luckily, we still have the beard hats, but the crowd from the concert has already filtered through. It's so late on a holiday, most people are tucked up inside and the ride uptown is quiet.

We're all worn out from a busy day. Barney slumps in the seat and it's all I can do to keep from wrapping my arm around him. Marci sticks to his other side and other than asking if he wants anything to eat, she's quiet too.

We emerge on 79th Street to nothing less than a winter wonderland. Everything is blanketed in a heavy pile of snow. We laugh and slip and trudge our way up the block.

I don't know who throws the first snowball, but halfway to the hotel it turns into all out war. It's the three other security guys against me, Marci, and Barney. Our shouts and laughter are muted in the heavy snow, and the wind whips away our words.

Maybe it was taking advantage of the situation, but I

definitely don't miss the opportunity to tackle Marci into a snowbank under the guise of trying to save her.

Then Barney pounces on top of us both like a goddamned flying squirrel and we collapse into a fit of breathless laughter.

It's all I can do to keep from kissing both of them.

We finally enter the lobby of the hotel all flushed and slushy.

Aside from a few glances from the front desk, we make it to the elevator and head up. The other guys are on the floor below Barney and I give them a fistbump when the doors open.

"Merry Christmas, guys," Barney says. His cheeks are pink from the cold. "Thanks for everything."

They leave with a chorus of goodnights.

No one questions when I stay on. It's my job to see Barney safely to his door and do a sweep to make sure his room is clear.

The doors shut and the elevator takes off.

It's the longest ride ever. We're all on separate walls, and the unresolved sexual tension is positively stifling.

Barney keeps his eyes fixed on the door, like he's trying to will them open faster.

Marci and I keep our eyes on each other. Everything we've all been unwittingly fighting against for years is about to finally blossom into something more.

The elevator dings and Barney's out like a rocket.

He's bouncing on his toes by the door while Marci and I catch up. We still don't talk. There are no words for this.

Marci gets the door open and I follow them inside.

The door shuts with a heavy click at my back.

They're breathless and beautiful. I spring an immediate hard-on and almost come right then in my fucking pants.

"You look cold, Barney." I meet his gaze and hold it. "I think you could use a bubble bath."

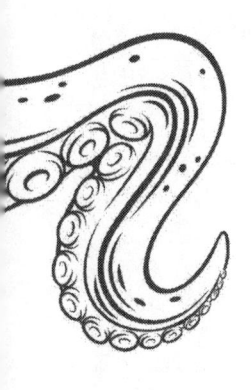

CHAPTER FOURTEEN

THE ROCKSTAR

I ALMOST CHOKE on my own tongue.

Marci heads into the bathroom. Ryder is looking at me so hard I'm pretty sure he's about to tackle me.

My heart races as he strides up and grabs my shoulders. Then he spins me and marches me into the bathroom.

The water's running and Marci's pouring in my bubble bath.

"Um." My throat dries. Knees wobble as I fight the instinct to dive into the tub. "What about a shower. We could—"

"It's okay, Barney." Marci turns and screws the lid back on the bottle. "We saw you."

"Wha—" I lean back against the counter. "*How?*"

Ryder hikes his thumb to a spot behind the tub. There's a window there looking into the bedroom. I hadn't even noticed it before.

Oh. Shit.

My breath rushes out. After all these years, I finally

slipped up. The blood drains from my head and the room sways. Marci's there in front of me. Her hands slide up along my cheeks.

"Hey," she murmurs. "It's okay. You're safe with us."

I glance over to Ryder and he nods. "We don't have to do anything you're not comfortable with. We can take things slow."

Marci moves her thumb along my cheek and smiles. "If we're going to be with you, though, we want to be with *all* of you."

It's almost too much.

My wish swells up to bursting inside of me and my eyes sting. Marci's face smears into a blur and my lower lip trembles. She kisses me, slow and soft, just simply brushing her lips against mine until my breath hitches.

I go limp under her grasp, and Ryder steps over to squeeze my hand. Marci pulls back and clears my face. I suck in a deep breath and let out a shaky sigh of relief.

Ryder plays with my fingers, swirling his thumb along the center of my palm. "Just so this is clear, before we get started... we're all here for sex, right?"

Marci jerks her chin toward Ryder, but doesn't take her eyes off mine. "He knows all about group sex, apparently."

"Hey, consent is important," he says.

"You're totally right." She runs her hand up his chest. "I'm not making fun. I think it's hot. And yeah, I'm here for all the sex."

"Me too." I nod emphatically. "I want to fuck both of you. I want to watch you fuck each other. I want you both to fuck me. Whatever order that all happens in, I don't care."

"All of the fucking. Got it." Ryder combs his fingers through my hair, running tingles throughout my body. "Any hard limits? I don't like choking, or anything around my neck."

"I don't like teeth or biting," I tell them.

"No derogatory names for me," Marci says. "I know it's hot for some people, but I don't like being called a slut or a whore."

I frown. She's so sweet, and kind, and thoughtful. I can't imagine anyone ever referring to her that way, even in play. "Has anyone ever said that to you?"

"A guy in college tried it." Her eyes spark. "Once."

Ryder's eyebrows shoot up. "Does he still have his balls?"

She smirks. "One of them."

"Noted." He rubs his palm up and down her back. "Red, yellow, green?"

"Red, yellow, green, what?" I ask.

"It's a system to make sure we're all on the same page once we get into it," Ryder says. "Green means we're all good. Yellow is for slow down. Red means hard stop. It's just an extra failsafe if anything gets to be too fast, or too much, or we need a break."

"Speaking of failsafe," Marci points to herself. "I've got an implant and I was all good on my last checkup."

"Negative on my last test," Ryder says.

"I'm all set, too." I rub the back of my neck and blush. "You both know how long it's been since I've gotten laid."

"Yeah." Marci's hands sweep up under my shirt, and

my stomach flutters. "We're definitely gonna make up for lost time on that."

She tugs and I lift my arms. My shirt is up over my head and tossed aside. Marcy trails her lips down the line of my chest while Ryder palms my cheek.

I'm instantly lost in his deep brown gaze.

"What do you want to do first?" He cups my chin. His lower lip juts out, so full and kissable.

"Kiss you." My voice is strained and reedy.

In a split second Ryder's on my mouth, working his tongue past my lips. I open for him and he plunges in, devouring me, stealing my breath.

I grip the edge of the counter and moan into his mouth. Everything about him is big and thick.

Marci's hands work at my waist, opening my jeans. She traces my human form through the boxer briefs, skimming small, clever fingers over the outline of my straining cock.

Ryder palms my waist. His thumb runs soft sweeping strokes right beneath my ribs. It tickles and I grab his bicep. It's like trying to wrap my hand around a tree trunk.

My senses explode. My brain short circuits.

I'm naked now, but I don't know how that happened. Marci's licking where my balls join the base of my cock. Her hand is wrapped around my shaft. It pulses as she squeezes and strokes.

I cry out and my knees sag. The only thing keeping me from collapsing is my iron-clad grip on the counter, and Ryder's iron-clad grip on me.

Pressure builds and builds until I can't stand it

anymore. The steam from the tub is turning the room foggy and humid. The sound of the running water fills my ears.

I need relief.

I tear away from Ryder, gasping for air. Marci looks up at me, eyes wide and questioning.

I groan and extricate myself from them, stumbling over to the humongous tub. The bubbles are halfway up the side, already piled high. I take a deep breath and slide into the water.

The change takes place immediately. I shut my eyes and shiver. A groan rumbles up from deep within me.

No human has ever seen me like this before. Then I remind myself that these two already have. They've seen the real me and they wanted all of it.

I let out a long breath. Slowly, I open my eyes.

My tentacles swirl in the steaming water around me, dipping and curling. I can feel everything through my suckers: the liquid motion of the water, the smooth marble of the tub, the soft tingle of the bubbles. It all adds up to a riot of sensation.

Ryder's arms are wrapped around Marci from behind. Her fingers stroke up and down his roped forearms as they watch me. Desire dilates their pupils and I've never felt so wanted before.

"Sooo..." I raise a tentacle and beckon them forward. "You wanna come in?"

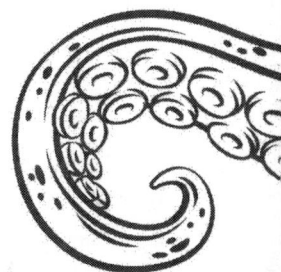

CHAPTER FIFTEEN

THE MANAGER

I YANK down my pants and pull off my shirt with shaking hands.

Ryder hops on one foot while he tries to kick out of his jeans.

Barney watches our little strip show with pure lust in his eyes.

I capture my hair and use the covered band I keep around my wrist to throw my curls into a messy bun on top of my head. The humidity coils tendrils around my face and along the nape of my neck.

My nipples are already peaked and my breasts ache with need. I squeeze my thighs together as Ryder steps up. He smooths his palm down my lower back and scoops up a handful of my ass.

His cock bobs soft and warm against my side. It's just as big as the rest of him. Like a fucking thoroughbred.

"Holy fuck," I whisper.

A drop of shimmering precum forms at the tip and

smears across my belly. I run my hand down his rippling length while he tests the weight of my breast in his palm.

I can hardly believe this is happening.

All those times I had to stop myself from staring at the wide expanse of Ryder's chest. All those times I had to avoid dance rehearsals just so I wouldn't drool over the way Barney moves his hips.

Now they're here looking at me like *I'm* the snack they're craving. My body floods with heat. The insides of my thighs get slick.

Barney's tentacle stretches out and curves around my back. It's warm and smooth and gentle as it grips my waist and pulls me closer. Another one curls around Ryder's muscular thigh. A prehensile tip plays with the bulging head of his cock. He leans forward with a loud groan.

I take Barney's hand and he helps me over the edge of the tub. Ryder slides in after me. The water rises almost to overflowing.

Tentacles surround my body, wet and smooth. One slips between my legs. I straddle the top of the undulating muscle as it presses up against my slit, pulsing with the same slick heat as my pussy. I wrap my arms around Barney's neck and press my lips to his. The tip of his tongue flicks into my mouth. I groan, and take him deeper.

His heart pounds against my chest. The bubbles fizz. I swear I can hear a rhythm in the two sounds.

Ryder grabs my breast again, kneading in time with the undulating tentacle between my legs. The smooth flat appendage feels like a giant tongue, spreading my body wide open. It curves up between my ass cheeks. A low, heady sound rises up my throat.

Lithe fingers curve around the nape of my neck, tugging at my hair. I pull back, drunk on Barney's kisses. I rock against his tentacle, searching for greater friction. His lips are swollen and pink. I love that I'm the one who made them look like that.

Ryder burrows his face into my neck. He nips at my earlobe, then sucks it into his mouth. I tilt to give him access. He runs the tip of his tongue down my neck, over my pulse.

Can he taste how my heart is vibrating?

He thrusts his hips forward with a gasp. I reach down and trace the tentacle curled around the full length of his cock.

"Is that okay?" Barney asks softly.

"Yes. Oh, fuck." Ryder's head falls back. His eyes shutter. His mouth drifts open. His wide arms span the huge tub like wings.

I stare at his sculpted abs as they twitch and flutter.

I stare so hard I forget to move my own body. Ryder grunts and goosebumps spread across his chest. I squeeze the base of the tentacle wrapped around his dick.

"Hang on," I tell Barney. "Don't make him come yet."

The tentacle unravels in an instant. Ryder sloshes back against the curved side of the tub. He shivers. His chest heaves while he tries to catch his breath.

"That's... fuck. I need a minute." He runs a wet hand over his hair. His eyes open, twinkling wickedly. "Why don't we find out what makes Marci moan?"

Barney arches a dark brow. "Good idea."

Tentacles coil around my thighs, little suckers feeling like a hundred kisses along my skin. They tug my legs wide, and I grab onto Barney's shoulders for balance.

Ryder sits back with a smug grin and watches, stroking himself lightly.

"How do you like it?" Barney asks. The tip of another tentacle prods my center. "Front?"

Another tip wiggles down my crack and nudges my rear. "Or back?"

"I—oh!" My breath catches and I bite down on my lower lip. "Both."

"Good." Barney slides his wide tip inside me.

I breathe slowly and remind my body to relax as it stretches around his girth.

"You're so hot, Marce." Barney toys with my peaked nipple while he edges inside. Behind me, the second tip circles my tighter hole. I dig my fingers into his shoulders and try not to scream.

"Hey." Ryder runs his warm hand up and down my back. "You got this. Just relax, baby."

I thread my fingers through Barney's lush hair and draw him to my chest. He buries his face in my breasts and sucks on my nipple in long circular strokes.

Ryder thumbs my other one, giving it gentle squeezes that coincide with the rise and fall of Barney's head. The tension seeps out of my body. My muscles ease.

Barney slides further inside me. One of the suckers latches onto my clit. The tentacles around my thighs undulate with a gentle pulsing rhythm. It feels like heaven. I release a full throated moan.

Barney sucks harder on my nipple.

He shoves further into me. The pressure builds. The tip circling my back entrance presses harder. Ryder's fingertips are right there at the edge.

"Good girl." He kisses my shoulder. "Next time you breathe out, push against him."

My forehead crinkles in concentration. Barney lifts his face and watches, running his fingertips along the edge of my jaw. I suck a deep breath through my nose, then arch my back. As I breathe out, I push. Barney's slick fullness slides right in.

I choke on my next breath. "Wow."

"Too much?" Ryder asks.

The stretch burns, arousing me in new, exciting ways. "No. It's good. So fucking good."

Barney lets out a rough sound and yanks my face down. He devours me like he's starving, diving into my mouth and my pussy and my ass all at once.

"You're fucking gorgeous, Marci," Barney murmurs into my mouth. One more languid sweep across my tongue and he's tearing away, panting.

His eyes zero in on Ryder. He yanks his head down until their noses are touching.

"Fuck me," Barney begs him. "Put your cock in me. I wanna come with her. Please."

CHAPTER SIXTEEN

THE BODYGUARD

BARNEY SNATCHES my wrist and plunges my hand under the water.

I let my fingers explore. The tentacles lead up to a smooth expanse of skin that culminates in a narrow hole. I circle the edge with my middle finger. It feels soft and wet, just like Marci's pussy.

My cock flexes.

Barney hums way back in his throat. "Yes. Right there."

I slide my finger in. The walls are slick and soft, textured with thin ridges. Barney's body clenches, swallowing my finger deeper. My cock throbs with urgent need.

Marci gasps.

She's in her own world right now, head thrown back, eyelids fluttering as she edges toward climax.

"Ryder," Barney pleads. His jaw is slack, his lips parted. His voice is desperate. "I need you."

Those words unleash something inside me. All of my

protective instincts take over. Passion burns through me, so hot and fast I nearly explode right then.

"I've got you, Barney." It comes out a growl. I capture his face, delving into his mouth in long, firm strokes. "Take what you need, baby. I'm right here."

His hand closes around my raging dick. It's all I can do to hold back as he guides me to his entrance. I remember how tight and textured he is, and choke back a shout.

Then my tip slides against his smoothness. Marci digs her fingers into my bicep.

Barney's eyes glaze. He lets out a whimper as I thrust in; just the tip. I start to pull out and thrust again, but the ridges lock onto my head and swallow me in.

"Holy mackerel," Barney mutters. "So big."

I exhale in a rush. "So tight."

Marci makes a sound somewhere between a moan and a whimper. Barney slings one arm around her waist and hauls her against his side while I smash into him from the front.

"I wanna come." Marci's hand flexes where she's still gripping my arm. A delicious flush stains her cheeks. "I need to—please."

"Almost there." Barney presses his lips to her forehead. "So close."

I use Barney's hip bone to keep him balanced while he takes me in all the way to the hilt. His silky skin caresses my balls. His body undulates around my length.

It's pure magic, the three of us all tangled together like this. I'm so blissed out, I don't even know what's me and what's them anymore. We're one big, writhing ball of pleasure.

Barney's pulsing around me. Then Marci's screaming and clawing my arm. Water sloshes over the edge of the tub. I brace my foot against the side and lunge up into Barney. Tentacles wrap around my waist and my thighs, sucking at my ass.

He squeezes tight.

Marci screams over and over again. Raw and unbridled.

"Yes! Yes!" Barney chokes out a sound that's raw lust.

The sting builds inside me. I crest and explode my release in hot gushing pumps. Barney's body convulses around me, like a throat swallowing down my cum.

We melt together in a spent pile of tangled limbs and tentacles. Barney shivers beneath me, squeezing one last drop of cum from my cock before going soft around me. I slide out, gasping for air.

It feels like my chest might collapse. At this moment, I don't give a shit if it does.

Marci melts, completely limp. The water has turned her bright curls a darker auburn, plastering them in a swirling mess against her skin. Somehow I manage to lift my arm and run my thumb along her cheek.

Her eyelids flicker open for a second. Her mouth turns up in a smile.

Barney's eyes are open, but far away. I don't think he exists on this plane right now. I scoop my other arm around him, cradling his head against my shoulder. He snuggles up without a struggle. I smooth the damp hair away from his forehead and place a kiss on his wet skin.

"It's perfect," he mumbles against my chest.

"What's perfect, baby?" I keep combing my fingers through his hair as he relaxes further against me.

"This. Us." He sighs and I feel him stamp a smile on my skin. "My wish came true."

I'm about to ask him what wish, but his hand slides down my stomach in a limp little splash and he falls into the release of sleep. Marci's body is slack against him, too.

I ease back and bring them into me, legs straddling them both. I grin, breathing out a long sigh as it hits me.

This is exactly what I wished for too.

CHAPTER SEVENTEEN

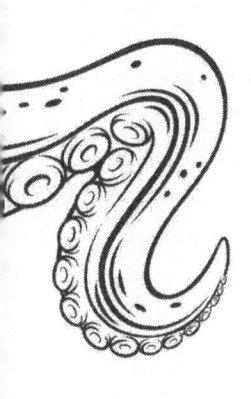

THE ROCKSTAR

WE REST TOGETHER in a haze of ecstasy until the water cools and I shiver.

I don't want to leave this moment. This is the only thing I want for the rest of forever. I want to wrap up these two humans who did the most unexpected thing and accepted every part of me, and place them under the Christmas tree as a gift to myself.

A lump forms in my throat and I snuggle into Ryder's side. He gives me a gentle squeeze.

Marci idly strokes one of my tentacles. The water is milky now, the bubbles long since gone, but none of us seem willing or able to move.

At last, Marci holds up her hands. "My fingers are pruny." She looks at me. Her eyes soften with concern. "Are you able to stay like this out of the water?"

"For a little while." Heat flares in my cheeks, and suddenly I feel shy. "You really like this better than my human form?"

I lift a tentacle and waggle it in the air. She grabs it

and kisses the tip. "There's no better or worse. I love everything you are, Barney, whatever form that takes."

My heart stutters. Ryder's arm tightens around me.

"You... love me?" I stare. Is this really real?

"Of course I do." Marci's eyes twinkle. "You think I'd trudge out into the freezing cold first thing in the morning to get coffee for just anybody?"

She traces the line of my jaw with the tip of her finger. Her eyes are deep and green and I see the truth there.

It's the same way she's always looked at me, I just never understood what it meant before.

"Marci—" She covers my mouth with her thumb, cutting me off.

"You don't have to say anything. Just enjoy it." She holds her thumb still until I nod, then lets it drop.

I glance up at Ryder. He's got that same mushy look in his eyes. How did I seriously not get this before?

Marci climbs out of the tub first. I hitch a piggyback with Ryder, wrapping my arms around his wide shoulders, molding my chest against the heat of his chiseled back. My tentacles grip his waist.

We go to the king-sized bed and Marci pulls back the covers. I crawl into the center, propping my back against the pillows with my tentacles fanned out.

"Come here, you." I open my arms for Marci. She gets on her hands and knees and follows my directions.

Craving overwhelms me again.

Ryder inhales sharply, eyes fixed on the voluptuous curve of her ass. My gaze drops to the sway of her breasts. I'm already trying to figure out how to keep them both naked in this bed and never do anything else ever again.

She kisses me, the sweet taste of her winding into me like expensive liquor. Her tongue is small and eager. I let her explore as we slide back and forth against each other, my tentacle tracing up and down the back of her thigh.

I crack open one eye. Ryder is watching us. He's already growing again, cock semi-hard and bobbing between his legs.

I lift my chin and nudge out of the kiss with Marci. "Turn around, baby."

I spread my tentacles and she settles against my chest. Her head falls back onto my shoulder. I bask in how easily she relaxes into my arms.

Ryder soaks up the sight of her pale, freckled body stretched out across the crisp white sheets. He licks his lips like he's just walked in on a full buffet.

"You hungry, Ryder?" I reach around and play with Marci's soft nipple, teasing it into a peak. "You look hungry."

His gaze wanders down between her legs. "Mm. I could go for a tasty little snack."

Marci wiggles her ass up against my waist and flexes her thighs. I graze her ear with my lips. "Did you hear that? Ryder's hungry. I think we should let him feast on you. Is that what you want?"

She nods and wriggles a little more.

Ryder leans forward on the bed.

"Out loud." He tucks a finger beneath her chin. "Look at me and tell me what you want, sweetheart."

At the authority in his voice, my insides go soft and melty. My tentacles suddenly feel extra sensitive.

"I want you to eat me out." Marci's belly trembles. She arches her back, pressing her breast into my hand even harder. I give her a little squeeze. "Please."

"That's a good girl." Ryder tweaks her other nipple with a sharp jerk and she slams her hips back into me.

Ryder glances at me and winks. I smirk and kiss her cheek, then curl my tentacles around her thighs. She holds tight. I push between her legs, capturing her quickly. I adhere my suckers to her soft skin and pry her legs apart, lifting them so her knees are splayed wide and open.

I reach out one of my tips and cover her clit with a sucker. She's warm and slick and I revel in her pleasure. It courses through me, every little touch and pulse and twitch of her body melting me from the inside out.

She's completely exposed between us. I can tell by the glint in Ryder's eyes she's eager and ready.

"So fucking drenched." He crawls up between her legs. "Mm. You must really want my face on your pussy."

She moans. "Yes."

He traces the crux of her thigh with his tongue. The silky pressure swipes along my tentacle, lingering just long enough to make me suck in a breath. "Here?"

"No." Marci wiggles her ass again, but I've got a tight grip on her. Hands flail wildly at her sides. Finally she grabs the sheets, digging her fingers into the plush mattress.

"This the right spot?" Ryder licks up long and slow on the other side.

Marci rolls her head on my shoulder. I grit my teeth, loving the sweet torture of it all. I increase the pressure on her clit while she strains against my grip.

She's strong and fierce, but she's no match for my eight tentacles.

"Damn it, Ryder." Her voice comes out ragged. She thrashes in my arms. "Eat my fucking pussy!"

He erupts in a low chuckle.

"Yes, goddess."

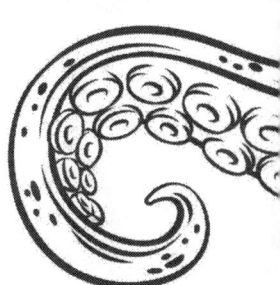

CHAPTER EIGHTEEN

THE MANAGER

RYDER DEVOURS ME.

That's the only word for it. He's relentless.

And holy fuck it feels good.

He dives deep into my pussy with his tongue, using long strokes and short strokes, alternating fast and slow. I can't predict what he's going to do next. There's no reason or rhythm.

Only his mouth.

It doesn't feel like long before he has me positively writhing. Barney is lanky, but damn he's strong. He holds my arms and legs, tossing and turning with me as I judder my hips, desperate to get more friction from Ryder.

It's infuriating. I love it. I'd suffer this sweet torture every day and get in line for seconds.

"More," I plead. "I need more."

Ryder stops. I'm left a breathless, heaving mess.

"Wha—?" I hear the quiet snick of a bottle and open my eyes.

Ryder balances a generous portion of clear lube on his middle two fingers. He reaches between my legs. I flinch as cold hits my ass.

"Sorry." Ryder doesn't look very apologetic. He massages my rear entrance in steady, gentle circles, so different from the wild way he was just attacking me with his tongue. "How's that?"

"Good," I sigh. My body softens beneath his expert touch.

Ryder hands the bottle to me. Without removing his fingers, he swings around and straddles my waist. He leans forward, and Barney and I are presented with the view of his perfectly rounded and muscular ass.

He's pure muscle, not an ounce of fat on him. His thighs are roped and powerful. I can't help but gawk.

Barney reaches up and runs a hand up and down Ryder's thigh, then tests the tightness of his ass with a little slap. Ryder's hips sway. He turns to talk over his shoulder.

"You two work on me. When we're ready, Barney's going to take us both from the back, and I'm going to fuck your pussy with my cock, Marci."

"Yes." My pussy gushes at the mere idea of it.

Barney's breathing stutters. "Okay."

I lift the bottle and squeeze a generous amount of lube at the top of Ryder's crack. It rolls down, and I nearly go cross eyed.

Barney catches it and smears it along Ryder's hole. Ryder groans. Barney gives his ass a firm swat with his tentacle: first one cheek, then the other. Ryder's hole jumps. The suction cups make a popping noise when they disengage, leaving a line of perfect red circles on Ryder's skin.

The three of us moan.

I didn't realize exactly how slick the water had made Barney, but now that he's drying out, the lube is necessary to smooth things along. I take some more and start working it up and down one of his tentacles. With my other hand, I play with Ryder's ass.

Barney and I work our fingers in just as Ryder slips two fingers inside me. Our varying noises of delight and pleasure blend together in sinful harmony. Barney and I massage in opposite directions, gently stretching and softening Ryder's entrance while he thrusts in and scissors mine.

The climb to ecstasy is slow and steady. Soon enough, we're panting and eager for more.

Ryder turns around and kneels between my thighs. He grasps the tentacle I've been working with lube and positions it between his legs. His cock stands up, bobbing against the rock wall of his abs. A thin streak of pre-cum trails out. I lick my lips, eager for a taste.

I can tell the moment Barney enters him. His eyes flutter and roll up into his head. A curse rumbles in his chest.

Barney's heart beats wildly between my shoulder blades. His heavy breath flutters the loose curls at the edge of my face.

Then it's my turn.

Barney's tip prods my entrance for only a moment

before he fills me. My jaw falls slack as my body fights to accommodate his fullness. Each sucker adds an extra layer of awareness.

Ryder hunches his shoulders and drops his head forward with a soft keening sound.

Or maybe that's me.

I can't tell which way is up anymore. All I know is that my pussy aches. I'm slick and dripping.

I need Ryder's cock.

It's like he can hear my thoughts. With a deep breath, Ryder lowers his hips and settles his weight between my legs. Balancing carefully, he rubs the blunted tip of his bulging dick up and down my soaking wet seam.

A shudder rolls through me. My belly trembles.

His eyes find mine: one last silent check as he notches his cock at my entrance. I dip my chin in a nod.

Then I shout.

He fills me in one thrust, hitting my deepest part.

Barney cradles me as I arch my back. His hand settles across my forehead, holding me in place. My fingers entwine with his other hand.

It's too much and not enough at the same time.

This. God. This is what I didn't know I needed.

For so long I held back, never believing I could have either of these men. Now they're both inside me, so deep, so hard. I swear to fuck they're touching places I didn't even know existed.

I break open. Blinding euphoria floods my heart.

This is more than just physical. I already told Barney I loved him. I meant it. But this, now, here, is so much more.

It's transcendent.

I climb and climb, like Icarus toward the sun. Instead of melting, I hit it with a blinding explosion, dissolving into tiny droplets of bliss that flutter down like the snow outside.

CHAPTER NINETEEN

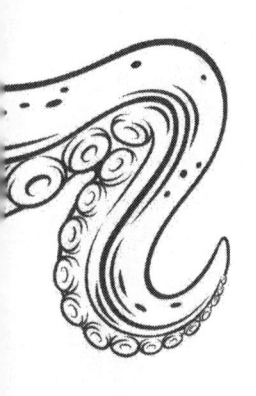

THE BODYGUARD

I COME BACK to consciousness in increments.

First I'm aware of the warm, tangled limbs. Then the soft gentle breaths.

I'm piled in a heap on the bed with Barney and Marci. My face is pillowed on Marci's thigh. My arm is slung over Barney's chest. His leg drapes over my waist.

I honestly don't even know if I have feet anymore. I don't really care. His tentacles are gone. I do know that. As much as I enjoyed the feeling of them around me, inside me, I can't be sorry for the form that's splayed before me now.

He's fucking gorgeous.

Long and lean. Sex and sinew.

Marci's breasts flatten gently across her chest, and I watch them rise and fall with each breath. I can't believe my luck. Fortune? Fate? Whatever the fuck it is that brought me to this place. Into these arms.

I'm hashtag motherfucking blessed.

My heart swells into my throat. I swallow back a

sudden wave of emotion. There's no doubt in my mind how I feel about these two. I'd go to the ends of the Earth for them. I'd do anything to keep them safe and close.

Forever.

I have no idea what lies in store for us after tonight. Whether we'll get fired, or what. But there's nothing that can keep us apart now. These two belong to me, and I belong to them.

Mine.

My jaw clenches.

I turn my head and kiss the supple skin of Marci's inner thigh. She wiggles and sighs under my touch. I reach out and trace the vee of Barney's waist. It points straight to his uncut cock, resting between his legs.

I trace light touches up and down his length, coaxing him to life. I shift so I can kiss and lick Marci, too, tasting myself mixed in with her. We make an intoxicating combination.

I smile at the thought.

Her eyes slide open. Her hand finds my hair, fingertips massaging my scalp.

"Mm. Like that," she murmurs.

"Yeah?" I whisper, adding extra breath to the end of the word. It dusts over her opening. Goosebumps pebble on her skin.

Her body wakes up, my own sexy, sinful Sleeping Beauty. She reaches out, then notices Barney is back to his human form. I slow down, giving her time to study him. The look on her face mirrors my own thoughts.

Marvelous.

She clears his silky hair away from his forehead,

smoothing her hand along his cheek, trailing down his chest, until his nipples tighten and he stirs awake.

We take things slow and soundless. We're in perfect sync, anticipating each other's needs. Lapping and loving on each other's bodies in turn, making sure no one goes unappeased.

It's soft.

Sensuous.

Perfect.

Barney curls up on his left side. I stretch out behind him while he rests on the pillow, nose to nose with Marci.

I lube his ass, placing soft kisses along his shoulder. Marci strokes his cock to fullness while mine grows against the base of his spine.

His eyes shutter. His breathing turns short and heavy. I glance over at Marci. She licks her lips, then nods and shifts to her back.

I guide Barney on top of her. He snuggles against her chest, kissing along her neck while he pumps his hips. I move behind them, and can't help but take a moment to watch.

His cock is slick, glistening with her arousal. He pumps in and out of her in slow, steady strokes. Her tight, pink hole stretches to accommodate him.

I run my palm over his ass to let him know I'm there. He sighs and ruts into her until he's balls deep, then holds still for me.

I line myself up to his waiting, eager hole and dip inside. We work in tandem; breathing, pushing, thrusting until I'm fully sheathed.

I blanket both of them with my body, careful to keep

my weight on my elbows. Marci rolls her hips. The motion ripples up through Barney and into me. After a few moments, we're in a solid and unrelenting rhythm.

Soaring into paradise.

My climax hits hard and fast. I pulse into Barney. He shakes beneath me, turning rigid while Marci clenches her thighs and screams.

I want to ride these waves into eternity.

CHAPTER TWENTY

THE ROCKSTAR

IT'S BEAUTIFUL.

It's perfect.

I can hardly contain my grin at how quickly and quietly this all came together. I was worried Marci and Ryder would wake up and ruin the surprise, but they're still snuggled up together in the bed, fast asleep.

We wore each other out and I'm not sorry about it.

No regrets.

Ten out of ten will definitely recommend.

For someone else, anyway. Ryder and Marci are all mine. No way am I gonna share them.

"Thanks! Merry Christmas," I whisper to the last of the hotel staff.

I hang onto the door, while they file out, closing it soundlessly behind them.

The living room of the suite has been turned into a magical wonderland. There's a huge fir tree in the corner. It's wrapped with twinkling white lights, decked out with frosted rose and gold ornaments. Tinsel dangles from all the branches, giving it a delicate wispy look. At the top gleams a bright star exactly like the one on the Rockefeller Tree.

I cover my mouth with my hand and squeal into my palm.

I tiptoe into the bedroom. It's dark with the heavy curtains still drawn, but I can see enough to crawl up onto the bed. My manager and bodyguard are curled up together like two contented cats.

They're so fucking cute I almost can't stand to wake them up, but I'm too excited.

I can't wait anymore.

"Marci. Ryder." I nudge them. "Hey, wake up."

They moan and groan, stretching and arching their bodies together as they wake up.

"The fuck Barn?" Marci mumbles.

"Time's it?" Ryder drags his hand down his face.

"You'll never guess what happened." I swallow a chuckle.

"Mmph." Marci yawns.

I shake them both. "Santa came last night!"

Ryder grunts. "So did the rest of us."

Marci buries her face in his chest and hides her laugh.

"Come oooon." I yank the covers back.

They whine and untangle themselves. I bounce back out to the living room, pacing back and forth between the couch and the coffee table.

Marci comes out matching me in the other fluffy hotel robe. She's rubbing her eyes and it takes her a second to notice the room.

Ryder's in a tight black t-shirt and his black boxer briefs. He bumps into her when she stops short.

Marci gapes. "Holy tinsel-splosion."

"Merry Christmas!" I throw my arms up in the air. "Ho! Ho! Ho!"

A huge smile cuts across Ryder's face. Marci just covers her mouth and shakes her head.

"Look." I retrieve the presents from under the tree. "I told you, Santa was here."

There's a box addressed to each of us 'from Santa,' wrapped in pink paper with gold glitter snowflakes spread across it.

Marci and Ryder join me on the couch, absolute delight plastered across their faces.

"Can we open them?" Marci asks.

"Duh." I yank the giant gossamer bow off mine and tear the paper away.

Marci and Ryder follow my lead.

"Barney, you didn't." Ryder stares down into his open box.

"Nope." I firm my mouth into a line to keep from smiling. "I had nothing to do with this. It was Santa."

Marci throws her head back and laughs. She pulls her white figure skates out of the box and holds them up next to Ryder's hockey skates. She peeks in and finds another pair of skates in my box.

I shrug. "I guess he heard we had season passes?"

"But—" Marci's shoulders drop. "We're based in L.A. How are we going to go to Rockefeller if we're all the way across the country?"

"Funny you should ask." I reach behind me to the

end table and pull out two smaller boxes. I place one in each of their hands. "This *is* from me."

Marci narrows her gaze. Ryder's cheeks turn a dusky rose. My heart jumps into my throat and I hold my breath.

I have no idea what they're going to say to this. I spent all morning thinking up a defense for every single argument I could imagine.

Marci unwraps her velvet box and opens it up. "A... key?"

I nod.

Ryder takes his out and examines it, then looks to me for an explanation.

"To our apartment." I swallow. "Here in New York."

Marci's face floods with emotion. "Barney...."

"It's just a lease for January," I plow in. "Rick says I have the month off. There's nowhere I'd rather be than here. No one I'd rather be with than you two. But if you don't want to—"

"Of course we want to," Ryder says. Marci swings around to look at him. "But we have contracts. We're all employed under the Gold Needle label and we're not allowed to fraternize with other employees."

"I know." I take a deep breath. "But if Rick wants another platinum record on the wall in his office, he's going to have to figure out how to make it happen. We've all proven over the past four years we can remain professional. I can either enjoy an inspiring relationship that will benefit the whole label, or I can let my fans know I'm leaving because I'm not allowed to love who I love. I think it'll be a pretty easy business decision."

"Wait..." Marci twirls her finger in the air. "Go back to the part where you mentioned love."

Now I'm the one blushing. "I love you. I'm in love with you. Both of you. Plain and simple."

"Me too." Marci smiles and shrugs. "As far as I'm concerned, you two are it for me."

"Same. I love you both so much." Ryder leans in and kisses Marci softly. He reaches over her and grabs my face, kissing me so tenderly it makes me dizzy. When he lets go, I turn and kiss Marci, too.

I stare at them in wonder, unable to figure out how this could be real. But it doesn't matter. The three of us are pure magic together.

My Christmas wish came true.

EPILOGUE
THE MANAGER

"EVERYTHING'S GREAT, MOM." I roll my eyes and glance around the crowded hotel lobby. The crew is all gathered, waiting for the buses to take us to the airport.

It's also check-in time and with the blizzard, rooms are still occupied so a lot of the guests are stuck waiting.

"We're going to London for the week and then I'll be spending January in New York," I tell my mom the good news. "Barney wants to stay here for his month off."

Barney leans in. "Will you bring us some cookies, Mrs. Collins?"

"Yes! I would love that! What a miracle. Santa couldn't have brought me a better gift!" I hold the phone away from my ear and glare at Barney. "Do *not* invite her over. She'll never leave!"

He laughs and steps away.

I roll my eyes and sigh while my mother goes off on a tangent making plans. The background noise at her house sounds just as chaotic as the lobby here.

Then the first strains of piano music drift across the

lobby. It sounds too clear and loud to be coming from speakers. It's something familiar in the style of Vince Guaraldi.

"Mom, I gotta go." I spin in a circle. Ryder and Barney have both vanished. Then I hear a clear, sweet voice.

Quiet ripples over the people as everyone notices the source of the music.

I hang up on my mom and follow the sound to the other side of the lobby. By the time I make it over, the entire room and all the people in it are dead silent.

All except for one.

Barney's belting out, "Holly Jolly Christmas."

Warmth spreads through my core. My ribcage feels like it might explode. I step over to Ryder who's next to the piano, watching Barney.

We keep a reasonable distance, but I feel him there, fingers brushing the back of my hand.

Then he surprises me by joining in the song. He's got a rich, deep baritone that blends perfectly with Barney's tenor.

Fuck it.

I start singing.

More voices trickle in. By the end of the song the entire lobby is belting out the words together. It's just like a Hallmark movie musical. Completely ridiculous, incredible, and so fun.

Rick Hartwell appears at my side. He leans in. "Think we could talk him into doing a holiday album?"

"Yeah." I can't help but laugh. "Pretty sure we could make that happen."

Somehow, the magic of Christmas has brought us all together, right here in this room. And Barney's joy has spread through each and every one of us.

I may not know everything the future holds, but I know one thing at least...

This is a holiday I'll never forget.

THANK YOU

Dear Reader,

I'm so grateful that you took the time to read *Tinsel & Tentacles*.

This book surprised me in a lot of ways. I was planning for it to be a lot shorter, but Barney, Marci, and Ryder all wiggled into my heart, and decided to get cozy for a little while.

I hope they found a special spot in your heart, too.

If you enjoyed reading this book as much as I enjoyed writing it, please consider leaving a review on Amazon and Goodreads.

Your review will be a gift to help other tentacle loving smutsters like yourself to find a book they enjoy.

Whatever and wherever you celebrate this holiday season, I wish you warmth, happiness, and love.

xxx Kate

ACKNOWLEDGMENTS

Thank you to my writing partner Laura. You always know how to talk me off the cliffs of insanity and make sense out of my tangled words. Go team!

Mikayla, you are my disco pumpkin goddess muse. Don't ever stop.

Special thanks to Romantically Inclined podcast, Tongue in Cheek podcast, and Tall, Dark, & Fictional podcast. Y'all helped me get the dishes done when they piled up from all this writing I've been doing. You also help me know I'm not alone in this wild and crazy smuttastic author journey and for that I'm very grateful.

I want to send extra love to my ARC team. Y'all really knocked it out of the park with this one. Your enthusiasm is my fuel, and you sent me to the moon and back!

And a big thank you to YOU my smutty reader. Thank you for taking a chance on this book. You are important and you are loved.

ABOUT THE AUTHOR

Kate McDarris is an emerging author of supernatural smut.

On Valentine's Day you can always find her picking out all the good chocolates out of the box before anyone else can get them.

Sign up for Kate's author newsletter at www.katemcdarris.com to stay up to date on all her latest releases, and be sure to let her know what you'd like to read about in her next smutty story!

MONSTER MASH HOLIDAY STORIES

A Fangsgiving to Remember

Leftovers are for quitters.

Melissa West spends her days pulling endless shots of espresso for her patrons at Books 'N Brews, and her nights living vicariously through the smutty fantasy novels she can't seem to get enough of.

When her bestie and roommate gets them into an exclusive Thanksgiving feast at a very swanky Upper East Side penthouse, Melissa's not so sure she wants to suffer through a blind date with a stranger.

Until she meets the stranger she's paired with: Mr. Tall Dark and Handsome, right out of her fantasies.

But there's more to him than meets the eye. He's packing a holiday surprise in his impeccably tailored pants, and he's going to give Melissa something to be thankful for. But will she survive until dessert?

Either way, it's a meal she'll never forget.

MORE BOOKS BY KATE MCDARRIS

My Billionaire Boss is a Vampire

"My boss is worth $42 billion. I just found out he's a vampire... and I'm about to be his next snack."

Alice has been crushing on her billionaire boss and there are definite vibes between them. One night she discovers the shocking truth he's been keeping: he's a vampire, and dawn is quickly approaching. Steric warns he'll do wicked things to her if she invites him inside. The sun might set him on fire, but Alice is the one he burns for.

He's standing in her doorway right now and she has a choice to make.

Does Alice have what it takes to survive a whole day alone with her billionaire vampire boss?

ALL THEY WANT FOR CHRISTMAS IS... TENTACLES.

THE MANAGER
Marci Collins has been crushing on her hot rockstar boss–and his equally hot bodyguard–for years. Now they're all in New York City for Christmas, and she only has one wish. It's just the chance she's been waiting for… but making a move might cost her everything and everyone she loves.

THE BODYGUARD
It's Ryder's job to put his body between danger and his rockstar client, but after years on guard duty, he's desperate to put his body on top of him… and his delicious manager. Always prepared for every situation, is he ready to take the ultimate risk to fulfill his deepest desires?

THE ROCKSTAR
World famous rock star Barney Myles needs a miracle. All he wants for Christmas are his manager and bodyguard underneath the mistletoe… but he's hiding a secret that could ruin his chances with them for good.

Little does he realize Marci and Ryder know more than he thinks, and they have a plan to make all their holiday fantasies come true.

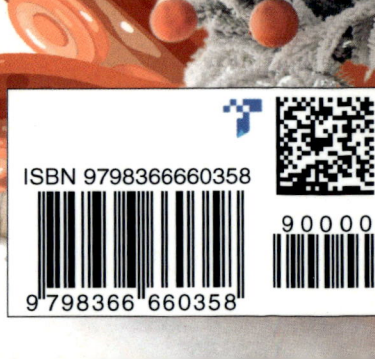

ISBN 9798366660358